MURDER

AT THE HOLIDAY HOME

Irish detectives investigate a peculiar homicide
in this gripping murder mystery

DAVID PEARSON

THE
BOOK
FOLKS

Paperback edition published by

The Book Folks

London, 2019

© David Pearson

ISBN 978-1-7986-3069-3

www.thebookfolks.com

For Betty, who has shown stoicism in adverse times.

Chapter One

Senior Detective Inspector Maureen Lyons awoke with a
start. It was pitch dark, save for the dull green glow
coming from the alarm clock on the night stand. It was
3:22 a.m.; Lyons turned over and instinctively reached out
across the cool white cotton sheets for Mick, her partner,
but her outstretched arm didn't find him.

Then she remembered. Detective Superintendent Mick
Hays had gone to Dublin for a meeting at Garda
Headquarters in Phoenix Park, and had been asked to join
the Commissioner along with a number of other senior
regional members of the force for dinner after the
meeting. He would have preferred to have come home,
but you didn't decline this type of invitation if you knew
what was good for you. The dinner would involve drink –
a lot of drink. When this gang got together, things could
easily go on well into the small hours, so Hays had booked
himself into the Aisling Hotel beside Heuston Station for
the night, or whatever portion of it would be left when the
revelry was over.

Lyons turned over. It was silly, and she knew it, but she missed him. Even for one night. Since she had moved in with him on a trial basis four years ago, they had become very close. She relied on him more than either of them realised, although she managed to feign independence extremely well – well enough to fool even herself most of the time. As she lay in their comfy king-sized bed, she thought to herself how well the relationship had actually worked. She had had doubts at first – after all, colleagues as partners was fraught with pitfalls of all sorts, but somehow, they had managed to avoid them, and they got along well both at work and away from it. The mutual respect that they had for each other's professionalism was certainly a large part of their success – both she and Hays were good detectives, and between them had solved some very challenging cases.

Lyons tossed and turned with sleep eluding her as the clock moved into the next green hour.

"Damn – this is no use," she said to herself, and turned on the bedside light, swung her legs out and wriggled her feet into her slippers. "I may as well get up, this is hopeless."

For the next three hours she busied herself tidying the already neat kitchen; ironing a couple of Mick's shirts, and hoovering the lounge, which, in truth, didn't need it. But she had to do something to pass the time. Eventually, at seven o'clock she yielded to the television to watch the early morning news on Sky.

The news was the usual mix of feckless politicians making excuses for the poor state of the health service; the housing crisis; the inexorable rise of crime, particularly in rural Ireland, and the usual array of vocal opposition members who seemed to have all the answers.

"Some things never change," Lyons said out loud, switching the thing off, and going upstairs to shower and get dressed.

* * *

It was just before eight o'clock when Lyons got to the Garda Station at Mill Street. The place had been recently refurbished and extended, so that now the Detective Unit, which had been based for over a year in an overflow building just down the road, was back in the main station again. It was a relief to have all the resources under one roof.

Lyons spent this somewhat quieter time before the normal hub-bub of daily tasks got underway, reading the many bulletins that had been posted by headquarters over the previous twenty-four hours. Most were purely informative, but one or two required a response, or some minor change to procedure which she would have to implement for her team of two detective Gardaí, a Detective Sergeant, and a less senior Inspector, as well as Garda John O'Connor, the unit's techy guy. Following the departure of Inspector James Bolger, the graduate entry officer who had joined the unit a year ago but didn't really fit in, Eamon Flynn had been made up to that rank, leaving a vacancy at Sergeant level which was yet to be filled. Her two junior detectives – Mary Costelloe and Liam Walsh – were not ready to be made up yet, so she was depending on Superintendent Mick Hays to find her a suitable candidate, and it was taking longer than she would have liked.

Lyons was engrossed in her work on the PC and didn't notice the time slip by, except that her own body was telling her it was time for coffee. As she locked the computer screen, the phone on her desk rang.

"Lyons," she said.

"Maureen, Maureen it's Séan here. Look, Maureen, we have a spot of bother out here."

Lyons immediately recognised the voice of Séan Mulholland, the Member in Charge of Clifden Garda Station. Although Lyons was now two ranks ahead of the sergeant, he still called her by her first name. At one time, they had both been sergeants together, and Mulholland never lost the habit; Lyons wasn't bothered in any case.

"Hi, Séan, what's up?"

"Peadar Tobin was called out to the cottages at Owen Glen earlier. There were reports of some odd goings-on. We thought it might have just been a break-in, or maybe a domestic, but it turns out it's far worse," Mulholland said.

Owen Glen was a small estate of twenty-eight holiday homes that had been built during the Celtic Tiger along the main Galway road, close to the Owenglin river, just two kilometres outside Clifden. They were a mixed bag of one, two, and three bedroomed houses with nicely pitched roofs and colourful front doors, tastefully spaced out in a large parkland area. They were originally priced at between a hundred and a hundred and fifty thousand euro, but since the crash, they had been selling for just a little more than half that, with many early buyers keen to realise their asset to settle other debts.

"Go on, Séan," Lyons said.

"Well, when he got there he found the front door of one of the houses up at the back – number twenty-two –

open, and the lights on inside. He tried to raise the occupier, but got no response, so he went inside, and he found a woman on the floor in the kitchen – God, Maureen, this is awful – and a large kitchen knife sticking up out of her chest with blood everywhere," Mulholland said.

"Jesus, Séan, he must have got a terrible shock. Was the woman dead?"

"She was indeed, at least as far as Peadar could tell. I sent two other men out and the ambulance of course, but I told them that if the woman was dead, not to touch her till you get here."

"Good man, thanks. OK, I'm on my way, and I'll get Sinéad Loughran out too with her team. Make sure to secure the area for us, Séan. See you soon."

"Oh, I will to be sure. Thanks, Maureen. See ye."

Lyons wasted no time in letting Sinéad Loughran know that she was needed out in Clifden. She asked Sinéad to call Dr Julian Dodd, the pathologist, and get him out there too. Then she summoned Inspector Eamon Flynn and Sergeant Sally Fahy, asked them to follow her out in one of their cars and gave them the address of where the victim had been found.

* * *

It was still before 10 a.m. as the detectives set off in their two separate vehicles. The sun had been up for some time, and was now quite high in the sky, peeking over the tall sycamore and pine trees that lined the road out to Clifden. Lyons was driving quickly, and when she had passed Moycullen she saw the unmistakeable large white 4x4 covered in bright yellow and red decals that she knew to belong to Loughran up ahead. Lyons had traded in her ageing Ford Focus earlier in the year, and was now the proud owner of a shiny, almost new, Volvo S60. Ever since she had borrowed Superintendent Finbarr Plunkett's Audi A6, she had been hankering after the luxury of cream leather and walnut. She eventually found it in a demonstrator at the local dealer, who had given her a generous allowance on the old Ford, even though it was, by that time, rather the worse for wear. Her new car had been fitted with a host of gadgets, courtesy of the Garda Technical Bureau, so that she could keep in touch with the entire force from anywhere in the country if required. It even had the latest Automatic Number Plate Recognition system installed, with a direct link to the Garda database of registered owners and stolen vehicles, although the system had not yet been connected to the insurance database, as it was in the UK, due to some data protection issue that had yet to be resolved.

As they made their way slowly through a traffic clogged Oughterard, Lyons spotted that Flynn and Fahy had fallen in behind her. There was still no sign of Dodd's Lexus, so Lyons called Loughran on the hands-free phone.

"Hi, Sinéad, I'm right behind you. Did you talk to Dodd? Is he on his way?"

"Hi, Maureen. Yes. He was in the middle of some ghastly procedure, but he said, as it was for you, he'd hurry up and be out shortly. I think he has a soft spot for you, Maureen," Loughran said mischievously, smiling to herself.

"Maybe when I'm dead, Sinéad, but not as long as I'm breathing. Thanks. Who have you got with you?" Lyons asked.

"Deirdre Mac and Tom Gillen," Loughran said.

Deirdre Mac, as she was known to everyone on the team to differentiate her from another girl with the same first name, was a highly experienced officer with a meticulous eye for detail. Gillen was young, and less experienced, but had learned a lot in the eighteen months he had been working with Loughran, and showed a good aptitude for forensic work.

When the little convoy reached the Owen Glen estate, it was clear that word had got out among the locals that there was something amiss. A small crowd of about ten people stood beside the entrance on the footpaths chatting and gossiping about what might be going on. There was no one from the press there yet, but the Gardaí knew that it was only a matter of time. Garda Peadar Tobin was manning a cordon of blue and white crime scene tape just inside the entrance to the complex, and he raised it up so that the cars could pass beneath. He noted the names of the new arrivals on his clipboard.

At the house itself, Garda Jim Dolan was standing on point at the front door. He greeted the team, relieved that someone more senior was now available to take over the macabre scene. Lyons got out of her car, and said to Fahy and Flynn who were just getting out of their own vehicle, "Right, you know the drill. Sally, can you take Jim here and start a house-to-house down the right-hand side; Eamon, you can go on your own down the left. I don't think there are too many of the houses occupied yet, so it shouldn't take too long. If anyone saw anything, stay with them and call me, I'll come down."

The two detectives acknowledged her orders, and set off in different directions. Lyons donned a white paper suit, gloves and overshoes, and followed Sinéad Loughran into the cottage, while the two other forensic officers started working the grounds immediately surrounding the house.

Lyons noticed that there were bloody marks along the wall of the short hallway at just above waist level, but they didn't prepare her for the shock of what she saw on entering the kitchen. Lyons had seen plenty of dead bodies in her time, but nothing like this. There, in the middle of the floor was the body of a woman who was probably in her late forties, lying on her back. She had short blonde hair and was dressed in a pink towelling dressing gown that had fallen open to reveal floral patterned cotton pyjamas. The woman's lifeless eyes stared out at her, still filled with the terror that she must have felt as she was being attacked and killed. In the middle of her chest, a large green-handled kitchen knife was sticking straight up, and her pyjamas and the floor all around her were covered in blood. She had something clenched in the left hand, but Lyons couldn't see clearly what it was, and she wasn't going to move anything till the forensic team had completed their grim task.

As Sinéad got to work around the body, the familiar booming voice of Julian Dodd was heard coming from the direction of the front door.

"In here, Doctor," Lyons said turning towards the entrance. A moment later, the diminutive figure of the bespectacled doctor appeared in the doorway. He was, as always, dressed as if he was going to a medical conference, with a starched white shirt, yellow tie and an expensive tweed suit and stout leather brogues. He carried his well-worn leather doctor's bag by his side.

"Ah, Ms Lyons. And what have you brought me all the way out here for today, may I ask?" he said, in his usual slightly pompous manner. Despite his superior attitude, Lyons had great respect for the good doctor who was amazingly thorough and had helped the detectives solve many a complex case over the years. Lyons thought his attitude was his way of compensating for his truncated stature, as she had always found him to be friendly and helpful beneath all the bluster.

"Good morning, Doc. See for yourself," she said indicating the prone form of the poor woman lying on the floor.

"Oh, dear me," the doctor said approaching the body, his attention now diverted to the business in hand.

Lyons stood by and waited while Dr Dodd examined the body as closely as the situation would allow. He had a small dictating machine in his left hand, and from time to time he spoke softly into it, as if he might disturb the poor woman's slumber. He moved to the side of the corpse away from Lyons, and gently peeled back the dressing gown from around the woman's throat. After a few more minutes of examination, he stood up wearily, and indicated to Lyons to step outside the room.

"Well, my word, what a puzzle you have brought me this time, Inspector."

"In what way, Doc?" Lyons said.

"Well, as you can see the woman had been stabbed in the chest. She is, for the record, dead, by the way."

"I had gathered that, Doc. But why is it a puzzle?"

"I can't be totally sure till I get her back to Galway, but I think she's been strangled too, and judging by the amount of blood all around, it looks to me as if strangulation occurred post-mortem."

"What? So, you're saying that she was stabbed to death with the knife and then strangled afterwards?" Lyons gasped, "but that doesn't make any sense at all. Why would a killer strangle her after she was already very obviously dead?"

"That, dear lady, is for you to figure out. I just certify death and try to help find out where and when. The rest is up to you," Dodd said.

"Speaking of which," Lyons said.

"Oh, I'd say roughly about 3 a.m. or thereabouts, or at least between one and four. Sinéad can take the knife, I don't need that, and then we'll get her back into Galway for a full post-mortem. It might have to wait till the morning though, I have something I need to finish up this afternoon," the doctor said.

"Oh, OK, thanks Doc. By the way, how was she strangled?" Lyons asked.

"A ligature of some sort. Not wire – something softer, maybe cord or fabric. Sinéad may be able to recover fibres from the creases in her neck, but that's her department."

"Right. Is that you done then?" Lyons said.

"Yes, that's it now, except that I need a cup of coffee. Coming?" Dodd said.

"No, you're fine. You go and get some in town. I need to stay here and organise things. I'll see you tomorrow."

Chapter Two

By the time Dodd had finished his examination of the body, Sally Fahy and Eamon Flynn had returned from the house-to-house that they had been carrying out.

"Well, did you get anything?" Lyons asked.

"There are only five houses occupied. One woman down near the front says she heard a car during the night, but she couldn't say what time it was, or give any other details, I'm afraid," Eamon Flynn said.

"Anything from your side, Sally?" Lyons said.

"No, sorry boss, nothing. I asked who owned number twenty-two though. The man wasn't too sure: he thought it was an Airbnb operation, and was owned by someone from Westport, but he didn't have a name. Did the woman have any ID on her?"

"No, not a scrap. No handbag, no papers, nothing to say who she is. I have Sinéad going through her clothes at the moment to see if she can see where the labels are from. That might give us a clue," Lyons said.

"Is there a car belonging to her around anywhere?" Flynn asked.

"Nothing obvious, Eamon. But can you have another look for me, and then maybe you two could go into town and ask the local estate agent if he knows who owns the house? I'm going to wait till the forensic team has finished, then we'd better get the body back into Galway. Dr Dodd is doing the post-mortem in the morning," Lyons said.

Lyons was walking back into the cottage when her phone rang.

"Hi you," Mick Hays said in a slightly gravelly voice.

"Oh, hi. You sound a bit hungover. How was it?"

"Late. I met up with that guy from Dungarvan, Fergal Mannion, you remember him, he was an inspector when we knew him last. Anyway, we got into reminiscing about the good old days, and it went on most of the night," Hays said.

"Helped along by a bottle of the best Irish whiskey, no doubt," Lyons said.

Hays didn't respond to the jibe.

"So, what are you up to?" Hays said.

Lyons told him what had happened and where she was.

"See. I can't leave you alone for more than five minutes before you go getting involved in all sorts of mischief. Need any help?"

"It's OK thanks, Superintendent. Why don't you go and have a nice greasy breakfast somewhere and then if you're sober enough, drive home? I'll catch you later."

"Good plan. I should be back around four or five. I'll go straight home, maybe catch up on some sleep," Hays said.

"Right. See you later then. Oh, and don't get pinged on the M6 – the local boys would just love that! Bye."

* * *

The forensic team continued with their painstaking work at the house. They dusted all the door jambs, handles and surfaces for fingerprints, and collected quite a few, although they had no idea if they were connected to the murder. They checked for dirty drinking glasses and cups from the dishwasher, taking them away for saliva examination later back at their lab. They examined the only bedroom that appeared to have been used, removing the bed linen for further exploration in Galway, and they collected up a number of personal items, such as a hairbrush, toothbrush and cosmetics from the en suite bathroom.

"God, that's gruesome," Sinéad Loughran said, holding up a clear plastic evidence bag containing the knife that she had taken from the woman's chest.

"Tell me about it. Are there any prints on it?" Lyons said.

"I'm going to wait till we get back into town to give it a good going over. I don't want to contaminate anything here. There might be, but then again…"

"We'd hardly be that lucky," Lyons said, finishing Sinéad's sentence for her.

"Exactly. We're about ready to remove the body now, if that's OK with you?" Loughran said.

"Yes, fine. Did you get anywhere with the labels on her clothes?"

"Just your average stuff, mostly M&S, but when we get her back to town I'll have a more thorough look – see where exactly they came from," Loughran said.

"Probably not local then. There's no M&S this side of Dublin as far as I know. But I'll get Séan Mulholland to check the mispers just in case. Thanks, Sinéad, I'll let you get on."

* * *

Eamon Flynn and Sally Fahy looked in the window of the estate agency belonging to Matthew Gilsenan on Clifden's main street, before going into the shop. They noticed that there were two houses in Owen Glen for sale, numbers five and sixteen, both with "Reduced" stamped across their details in red ink.

Inside, there was a man of about fifty years of age dressed in a mid-grey suit with a blue shirt and dark tie, seated at one of the two desks. He looked up as the two detectives entered, hoping that they were a couple about to make some significant purchase.

"Hello there. Nice morning, isn't it?" the man said cheerily, standing up and extending his hand to Eamon Flynn.

Flynn introduced himself and Sally, and Gilsenan's cheerful demeanour left him, his hopes dashed, even though he tried not to show it.

"How can I help you today, folks?" he said.

"We're investigating an incident out at Owen Glen, Mr Gilsenan. It's number twenty-two. Would you happen to know who owns that one?" Fahy said.

"I should do. We sold that whole estate after it was built in 2007. Let me see, twenty-two – I'll just look it up in the files. Won't be a moment," he said, turning his back briefly on the two detectives to rummage in a steel grey filing cabinet behind his desk.

"Owen Glen, Owen Glen – yes, here it is. Twenty-two. Sold for five grand below the asking price in 2007 to Batty McCutcheon, that is Mr Bartholomew McCutcheon. He's from Westport," Gilsenan said.

"And would you happen to have an address for Mr McCutcheon at all, sir?" Flynn said.

"I have. But he runs the shop there on the main street – Eurosaver, I think he calls it. You can't miss it. They sell all sorts of stuff – cosmetics, household goods, sweets, batteries – you know the kind of place, all bright colours and cheap stuff from China," he said.

"I see. Well, just in case, could you let us have his home address too, please? We might need to call on him," Fahy said.

Gilsenan obliged, and the two detectives thanked him for his time and assistance and left.

When they were gone a few minutes, Gilsenan lifted the phone and made a call.

"Batty, is that you? It's Matt here from Clifden. Look, I've had two coppers in here asking about you and that place you rent out up at Owen Glen. I think you can expect a visit sometime soon. I just thought you should know."

* * *

The body of the unknown victim was bagged and loaded into the anonymous black Mercedes van to be taken to the morgue attached to the regional hospital in Galway city where Dr Dodd would conduct the post-mortem the following morning.

The forensic team finished their grim work, and Garda Peadar Tobin was instructed to secure the premises. Sinéad Loughran chatted to Lyons outside the house as she removed her white paper suit, mask and overshoes. She flicked her blonde ponytail out from her jacket collar, and breathed a sigh of relief.

"Any initial thoughts?" Loughran said to Lyons.

"Not really, Sinéad. No sign of a struggle, but someone obviously didn't like her very much. It's very odd that she was strangled after she was stabbed. I haven't seen that before. After all, the killer clearly knew she was dead, and as far as I know, you can only die once! Will you be able to get any clues from her neck?" Lyons said.

"I hope so. Whatever he or she used will probably have left traces buried in the skin. But we'll have to see."

"Do you think it could have been done by a woman?" Lyons said.

"Possibly. I won't rule anything out till we know more. Where are you going now?"

"I'll stop by to see Séan. It's his patch after all."

As she was saying goodbye to Loughran, Lyons' phone rang. It was Sally Fahy giving an update on their visit to the estate agent.

"OK. Well, can you and Eamon get over to Westport and interview the owner of the house? Find out who he had it rented out to, and let me know as soon as you have any information. We need to find out who the victim was."

Chapter Three

"Ah, 'tis yourself Maureen. Come in and sit yourself down. I was just about to put the kettle on. Will ye have a cup of tea? You look fair worn out," Mulholland said.

"Thanks, Séan, that would be great," Lyons said, sitting down at a spare desk in the back office of the Clifden Garda station.

Mulholland busied himself making a nice big pot of tea, and returned a few minutes later carrying the teapot, a small jug of milk and two pottery mugs.

"Would you care for a little something in your tea, Maureen? It's a bad business this," Mulholland said, pouring Lyons' tea, but leaving plenty of room for a tot of whiskey.

"Just a drop then, Séan, thanks. I'm driving after all," Lyons said, grateful for the consideration of her colleague, who had his own particular set of procedures for these situations that weren't to be found in any instruction manual.

"Do you know anything about this McCutcheon character, Séan?" Lyons asked, sipping her reinforced tea.

"Well, a bit. He's some kind of big shot in Westport. Has that shop in the main street that sells all sorts of shite mostly from China. It does well though, by all accounts, especially since the crash. And he has a few properties around and about, including that one out in Owen Glen. I can get the lads out in Westport to give us a bit more if you need it," Mulholland said.

"Let's see what Eamon and Sally get out of him. He may not have anything to do with anything just because he owned the house. But we'll know more later."

"And what about you, Maureen. Are you OK?" Mulholland said.

"Ah, I don't know, Séan. Sometimes I think all this is a bit much for me. I know we've had more than our fair share of murders out here in the last few years, but they don't get any easier. Take this one, for example. We have no idea who this poor woman is, or what she was doing here. I'm a bit at a loss to be honest," Lyons said.

"But it's early days, Maureen. You haven't left one in the cold case file yet. It'll work out for you, wait till you see. And if there's anything at all we can do for you out here, just say the word."

"Thanks, Séan, that's helpful. Don't mind me, I didn't sleep well last night. I'll be fine," Lyons said.

"Are you going to set up the investigation out here in Clifden?" Mulholland asked.

"I don't think so, Séan. We'll need all the resources we can muster back in the city. But I'd say we'll be out and back quite a bit. Have to train my new car to drive the N59 by itself!" she said, feeling a bit cheerier. Mulholland may not have been the dynamic force that the Garda seemed to be demanding of its officers these days, but his heart was in the right place, and he was a good cop, and a decent man as well, Maureen reflected.

"Thanks for the pick-me-up, Séan, I'd better be away back to the city," Lyons said getting up to leave.

"Fair enough, Maureen. Mind how you go now. See you soon," said the sergeant, gathering up the dirty mugs and tidying away the three-quarters full whiskey bottle.

* * *

Sally Fahy and Eamon Flynn drove out along the N59 through Letterfrack, then on to Leenaun and into the Mayo town of Westport. In the midday sunshine, the scenery was breath-taking, and they took their time so that they could enjoy the magnificent views as they passed by the various lakes and imposing hills that surrounded them.

"What do you make of this lot?" Fahy said to Flynn.

"It's a right old mystery so far. Maybe McCutcheon will be able to tell us who she is and what she was doing there," Flynn said.

"Yeah, but even so, how did she get there? She didn't appear to have any transport, unless whoever killed her stole her car. And how come there was no paperwork anywhere? That's bizarre," Fahy said.

"And what about the way she was killed? Who the hell strangles someone after they have stabbed them? That's just weird."

"Do you think Maureen is up to it?" Flynn said.

"Yes, I do. And even if she has to get a bit of help from Hays, she'll crack it all right. Do you not agree?" Fahy said.

"We'll see. I know she's good, but this will test her mettle to the limit, wait till you see. Anyway, let's do as much as we can to help her out. It's not just her reputation that's at stake. The whole unit will come under scrutiny if we mess this up."

* * *

They found the Eurosaver shop in Westport easily – indeed you could hardly miss it. It was painted in gaudy bright yellow and red paint, with an enormous illuminated sign over the entire shop front. The window was festooned with large posters advertising this week's bargains, which did seem to be very cheap indeed.

Inside the shop, several young girls dressed in black trousers and black t-shirts, with the word 'STAFF' emblazoned in large white letters both front and back, were busy serving customers and stacking the shelves.

While Flynn browsed the merchandise, Sally Fahy approached one of the young girls busy packing cleaning products onto a shelf near the door. The girl was short, with long dark hair scraped back over her head and tied off with a hair band at the back.

"Excuse me, I'm looking for Mr McCutcheon," she said.

The girl stood up, displaying a name badge that identified her as Rami, and said, "I don't think he here today. Wait. I ask." She headed off down the back of the shop and through a door marked Staff Only. She was back a minute later.

"Mr McCutcheon's not here today. He working from home," Rami said rather sullenly, and went to go back to her task.

"Do you know where he lives?" Fahy said.

"No. You'll have to ask in the office."

"Thanks. Can you tell me where you are from?" Fahy asked.

"Lithuania, near Klaipeda, on the coast," the girl said.

"Do you enjoy working here?"

"It's OK. Pay is poor, but the boss rents us a room at a special price, so all good," Rami said, almost smiling.

"Hmm, OK. Where is the office then?" Fahy said.

"Down back. Staff door. Just knock, Mary will tell you. I have to work," the girl said and went back to stacking the shelves. Fahy got the impression that she was worked pretty hard. She would love to know exactly how much the girl was paid, and how much she was charged for rent. But that was for later, if at all. Right now, they had more important matters to attend to.

Fahy had to produce her warrant card to get Mary to confirm McCutcheon's address. He lived a little way outside the town on the coast road near Lecanvey.

"Go past the pub, and the church. Ignore the first turn to the right – that goes down to the pier. Then take the next on the right, and just down there before the holiday cottages, there's a bungalow on the left painted yellow – that's Mr McCutcheon's house," Mary said.

"Great, thanks. Could you just give him a call and make sure he'll be there in about twenty minutes?" Fahy said.

Mary made the call, and confirmed that her boss would be at home. He wanted to know what the unexpected visit was about, but Fahy just said that she would explain when they got there.

On the way out to Lecanvey, Flynn, who was driving said to Fahy, "How do you want to play this, Sally?"

"It's up to you, boss. What if you lead, and I have a bit of a snoop around and see what I can pick up from the house, or the wife, if she's there? Would that suit?"

"Yeah, OK, let's do it that way. Look, here's Lecanvey now. I presume that's the pub Mary was talking about, so it should be the second turn on the right after the church," Flynn said.

He slowed the car down to a crawl, they passed the church, which looked far too big for what must be a very small population in the village, and after a moment they came to a right hand turn with a brown sign pointing to "Lecanvey Holiday Cottages".

The road down to the cottages was no more than a track, with weeds growing in the middle of it, but it had at one time been tarmacked. Flynn turned the car onto the lane and almost immediately a large bungalow, standing on an elevated site, came into view. By contrast to the road, the driveway leading up to the house was immaculate. New tarmac had been laid, and the gardens that swept up to the house were neatly manicured with early summer flowers of various colours set out in orderly beds. A new and expensive Hyundai jeep stood on the drive outside the house, flanked by a three series BMW, also with a recent plate.

"McCutcheon does well for himself selling cheap Chinese tat," Fahy remarked as Flynn brought their scruffier vehicle to a halt.

"Doesn't he though," Flynn replied.

The bungalow had obviously been quite a modest affair at one time. It had the customary three arches adorning the front – just like almost every single dwelling built recently in the west of Ireland – but had been extended on both sides to turn it into a house of substance. Flynn knocked on the solid oak door and stood back.

The woman who opened the door was in her late forties. She was very well dressed, and her neat figure showed off her fashionable clothes to good effect. Her long straw-coloured hair was tied up behind her head, and her makeup was subtle and flattering. She spoke in a neutral, well-to-do accent.

"Good morning," she said, pulling the door wide to reveal a fully tiled hallway, "you must be the police that Mary called about. Come in, please," she said, standing back and ushering them into the hallway.

"We're in the kitchen. Can I get you tea or coffee?" the woman said, walking towards the back of the house.

"Thank you, a coffee would be lovely. What a nice house you've got," Fahy said.

"Yes, thanks, a coffee would be great," Flynn said, not quite sure if he should add some compliment too.

When they entered the kitchen, it immediately became clear just how much work had been done to the house to bring it to its current state. The entire back of the place had been made into an enormous kitchen diner, with modern units, the very latest in appliances, and a dining table with a sofa and two easy chairs further along in front of a generous open fire. All along the back wall, picture windows looking out onto the ocean had been installed, and the view down over the holiday chalets, across the rugged coast and on out to sea was extraordinary, made even more so by the sunny weather.

Bartholomew McCutcheon was seated at the table with a newspaper in front of him, and a large mug of coffee. He got up as the trio entered the room.

"Good morning, officers. Come in, take a seat. Eleanor will get you a hot drink," the man said. McCutcheon was from different stock than his rather gracious wife. He was a big man, with a large paunch protruding out and over the waist of his well-worn grey slacks being just about held in place by a creased, pale blue shirt. He had a ruddy, weather-beaten complexion, and a thinning crop of rather greasy grey hair scraped across his scalp. It appeared that he hadn't shaved.

Flynn sat down at the table, but Fahy stayed upright, and went to see if she could help Mrs McCutcheon with the drinks. Flynn noticed McCutcheon spent a little longer than was polite eyeing the shapely figure of the young Sally Fahy as she stood at the counter with her back to him.

"Thanks for seeing us, Mr McCutcheon. I'll get straight to the point so as not to waste your time. I understand you own a property out at Owen Glen, the far side of Clifden. Is that correct?" Flynn said.

"God, I do," the man replied in a thick Galway accent. "I paid way too much for it as well, but it's doing fine now, thank God."

"How do you mean?"

"Well, I rent it out, you know, on this new-fangled thing, Air-b whatsit. It's dead handy, though sometimes it's hard to get on-line from here, so I do have to go into Westport to get a connection," he said, looking a little nervously at his wife who was now arranging the drinks and some chocolate biscuits on the table.

"And is it rented out at present, Mr McCutcheon?" Flynn asked.

"Oh, God, no. 'Tis too early in the season. We sometimes get a few stragglers coming through around

Easter, but the real season starts when the kiddies get out of school in about two more weeks. Then it should be full for the summer," he said relishing the thought.

"And you're sure that it wasn't rented out last night?" Flynn persisted.

"I am. Why? What's happened?"

"I wonder if we could just have a look at your bookings on your PC, Mr McCutcheon?" Flynn said.

As McCutcheon got up to go and fetch his laptop, Fahy asked his wife, "I'm very sorry, Mrs McCutcheon, but I wonder if I could use your loo?"

"Of course. No problem, it's down the hall, second door on the right," she said.

McCutcheon returned carrying a swish Apple MacBook, opened the laptop and fired it up.

"We might not be able to get on, but let's see," he said, tapping the keys slowly with two pudgy fingers.

"Ah, here we are. Look, you can see for yourself. It's not booked till Friday week when we have a family of four coming for five days," he said pointing triumphantly to the screen.

"Hmmm. I see," Flynn said.

"Why? What's happened? Did it go on fire or something? I hope I remembered to renew the insurance," McCutcheon said.

"No, no, nothing like that, Mr McCutcheon. It's safe and sound. May I just ask you where you and your wife were last night?"

"Well, I got back from the shop around quarter to seven. We had dinner, and then I had to go back into Westport – I had a bit of business to attend to. Eleanor, did you go out at all?" McCutcheon said.

"No, of course not. I told you, Betty from the ICA was over. We're doing the arrangements for the summer fair in the village. It's on next month," Mrs McCutcheon said.

"Look, detective, what's all this about? What's happened?" McCutcheon said.

Flynn explained the sinister goings-on at 22 Owen Glen the previous night, much to the horror of the couple who looked visibly shocked by the news.

"Dear God in heaven, that's appalling. Do you know who the poor woman is?" McCutcheon said.

"No. We were rather hoping you might be able to throw some light on that for us," Flynn said, letting the sentence hang in the air.

"What? What do you mean?"

"Well, if she had been booked in, then we would be able to identify the woman at least. We found no identity of any kind on her, or in the house. Right now, we haven't a clue who she is or where she came from," Flynn said.

Fahy had come back into the room, and was standing with her back to the cupboards, leaning against the counter top, clutching her coffee mug. She noticed that McCutcheon was eyeing her up, getting a good look at her figure now that she had opened her jacket.

"Was the house broken into?" Mrs McCutcheon said.

"No, it doesn't appear to have been, which in itself is odd. Can you tell us who has keys, apart from yourselves?" Flynn said.

"Ah, sure don't ye know, half the world has keys to these holiday lets. They never return the bloody things when they leave. I spend my whole life getting new ones made. That Owen Glen place is worse than anywhere else too," McCutcheon said grumpily.

"But is there a cleaner, or a handyman that has keys?" Flynn asked.

"Oh, there is right enough. One of your fellas does a bit of work on the place if it needs something – Peadar Tobin he is. And there's Agnes Greely who does the cleaning after the guests have left. She lives in Owen Glen at number twelve. She's a widow, and the extra money comes in handy for her."

Flynn gently probed the McCutcheons for more information, but got nothing useful that could help with their enquiries. After another quarter of an hour, the detectives thanked them and left. McCutcheon asked if it would be OK to let the property if the opportunity arose, and Flynn told him that as it was a major crime scene at the moment, he should wait to hear from the Gardaí before allowing anyone near the place.

Chapter Four

It was well into the afternoon when Eamon Flynn and Sally Fahy had finished their interview with the McCutcheons, so they decided to drive straight back to Galway, and leave further enquiries until the next day. In any case, they would need to tell Senior Inspector Lyons about what they had been told concerning Peadar Tobin. That was an unwelcome complication.

On the way back in Flynn's car, they talked about the interview that had taken place.

"What did you make of all that?" Fahy asked.

"Interesting. McCutcheon certainly has a roving eye – did you see the way he was undressing you in his mind a few times?" Flynn said.

"Yes, I spotted that – creep. And I don't think they are sleeping together either," Fahy said.

"Oh. How do you figure that out?"

"When I went walk about, I glanced into the bedrooms. It looks like they have separate rooms, unless there's another woman living there, and I don't think there is," Fahy said.

"Well, would you like to wake up beside Mr Batty McCutcheon every morning?" Flynn said smiling.

Fahy swatted his leg, "Feck off, boss. No, I bloody wouldn't!"

* * *

When Lyons got home to Salthill, Hays was just waking up. She had gone upstairs to change out of her work clothes, and found him in bed, just coming around.

"Hi, hun. I fell asleep," he said.

"So I see. Feeling better?" she said, sitting down on the edge of the bed and kissing his cheek.

"Ooh, you need to brush your teeth," she said getting up to escape his bad breath.

"Damn. And there I was hoping," he said.

"Later, Superintendent, later. I need to eat. C'mon, get dressed, we're going out for food – my treat."

"Yes ma'am," he said, leaping up from the bed and heading to the bathroom.

Fifteen minutes later, Hays was showered and looked a lot fresher. Lyons had changed into one of her favourite light summer dresses, and looked radiant with her dark, shiny hair and big sparkling brown eyes.

"Where are we going?" Hays asked.

"Let's go out to Clarenbridge. I fancy some seafood."

"Mmmm oysters!"

"Behave, Superintendent," she said linking his arm as they walked out to his car.

The food in the restaurant in Clarenbridge was delicious, and when they had both tucked away their starters, Hays asked her, "So, what's the craic with this thing out west?"

"Bit of a mystery to be honest. We haven't identified the victim yet, and I'm not quite sure where to turn next. No one seems to have seen anything, and there was no ID at all on the body, or in the house. Any ideas?" Lyons asked.

"I have, as it happens. Why don't you do a 'Maureen Lyons' on it – get back out there? Soak up the place. Let your instincts talk to you. I bet you'll find something. You always do."

"Well, not always, but I know what you mean. Fancy a drive out west in the morning?" she said.

"I'm sorry, love, I can't. There's a budget meeting at ten that I have to attend. See what cut backs they want to impose on us this time. If I'm not there, we'll all end up on bicycles."

"Oh, right. I'll take Sally with me for company then. She's as sharp as a pin, you know."

"Yes, she is. And easy on the eye too!" Hays said.

"I thought you preferred brunettes."

"I do – well, one brunette in particular. Just teasing."

* * *

The following morning, Lyons held a briefing with the team before setting off to the post-mortem.

"Right, everyone, what have we got so far?"

Flynn and Fahy filled her in on the interview they had held with Mr and Mrs McCutcheon the previous day in Westport, except that no mention was made of Peadar Tobin's part-time job as maintenance man at the holiday let.

"Hmm, OK," she said. "Well, clearly we need to check out McCutcheon's alibi for the evening of the murder. He may have been with another woman, from what you say. So, Eamon, will you contact him at the shop and see what he has to say for himself, and then follow up on whatever information he gives you?"

"John, I'd like you to check out that Airbnb thing for the cottage. I'd like to get a list of people who rented it over the past several months. Let's see if there is any sort of a pattern to it. When I've finished at the post-mortem, I'm going back out to Owen Glen to have another look around, and I want you with me, Sally. Mary, you and Liam can open a murder book on the system and key in everything we have so far. I'll see Sinéad at the post-mortem and get anything her team might have found as well. Let's meet back at around five and compare notes, and remember, if anything significant comes up during the day, let me know immediately."

* * *

Dr Julian Dodd had the post-mortem well underway when Lyons arrived at the morgue. The classic Y shaped incision had been made into the woman's body, and the major organs had been removed.

"Ah, Inspector, good of you to join us. Come in," Dodd said in his usual slightly acidic tone.

"Morning, Doc. Anything of interest?" Lyons said as she approached the bright stainless steel gurney on which the woman was laid out. The dead woman had been pretty in life, with shoulder-length blonde hair showing slight signs of grey here and there. It looked as if she had been slim, or at least not heavy, although her bone structure was solid enough. Her pelvic area was covered with a cloth for the sake of modesty, but Lyons knew that there would be no part of this woman's body that Dodd would not explore in minute detail.

"Yes, well, a few things. I've managed to recover a few strands of the ligature that were buried in the folds of skin at the neck. Only small pieces mind you, but maybe enough for Sinéad to get a fix on what kind of stuff it was made from. The knife wound is pretty self-explanatory. One single incision that went straight to her heart with almost instant death. She was standing up when she was stabbed, and her assailant was maybe three or four inches taller than her."

"Can we assume it was a man?" Lyons said.

"You can assume whatever you like, Inspector. All I can say is that the person who stabbed her was a bit taller than she was. The attack wasn't frenzied, it was a single, measured stabbing. Sinéad is examining the knife as we speak," the doctor said.

"Any sign of sexual activity – was she raped?" Lyons asked.

"No, nothing that handy, I'm afraid."

"Anything else of note?" Lyons said.

"Not yet, but I'll be doing a full report later on and that will contain all the details."

"Very well, Doc, I'll let you get on. Oh, one more thing – had she eaten before she was killed?"

"Yes, she had. I'll give you the details in my report, but I'd say about three hours before her life ended, if that's any help."

"Thanks. I don't know to be honest, but it might be," Lyons said.

Lyons then went in search of Sinéad Loughran, and found her in the Pathology Lab upstairs, staring into a microscope.

"Hi, Sinéad. How's it going?" Lyons said.

"Oh, hi Maureen. Slowly, I'm afraid. What about you?"

"Ah, ye know. So, what have you for us then?" Lyons said.

"Well, I'm examining the tiny specs of the ligature that Dodd pulled out of the woman's neck. I think it's some kind of cotton fibre – not common these days," Loughran said.

"Maybe it's some kind of rope or picture cord?"

"No, I don't think so. All of these things are made from man-made fibres. But I haven't finished my examination yet. I'll let you know when I have done some more on it," Loughran said.

"OK, thanks. By the way, was there anything washed down the sink – any trace of drugs or anything?" Lyons said.

"We did look down the drains, as we always do. But Owen Glen is connected to the main drainage system and mains water – it was one of the big selling points when the houses were built. No messing about with septic tanks, or wells that could run dry in the summer. So you're out of luck there, I'm afraid."

"Terrific. Typical!" Lyons said. "And what about her handbag?"

"Didn't find one. I thought that strange too, but there was no sign, and we searched all over," Loughran said. "What are you up to now?"

"I'm going to go back out there as soon as I've finished here. Mick thinks the location might have more to give up.

I'm not sure, but it's better than sitting on my hands in any case."

"Oh, OK. Well, if I find out anything from here, I'll give you a call. Good luck," Loughran said, returning to her microscope.

Lyons collected Fahy and they set off from the city out west towards Clifden. When they were underway, Fahy broached the tender subject of Peadar Tobin.

"Boss, there's something you need to know," Fahy said.

"Oh, what's that then?"

"When we were interviewing McCutcheon yesterday, he told us that Peadar Tobin does some handyman work for him at Owen Glen – just maintenance things from time to time."

"Jesus, Sally. Why didn't you tell me earlier?" Lyons said.

"This is the first chance I've had where the whole station wouldn't hear about it. I thought you'd prefer it that way."

"It's bloody awkward. Wasn't he the first responder?" Lyons said.

"Yes, yes I think so."

"Christ, the whole case could be compromised if this gets out. You can just imagine what a decent defence barrister would make of that! You'd better keep this quiet and let me handle it – and tell Eamon to do the same. Will you both be OK with that?" Lyons said.

"Yes, of course. Mum's the word," Fahy said, and the two continued in a sombre silence until they reached Owen Glen.

"What's the plan?" Fahy said.

"I'm not sure. I want to start up at the cottage and walk down to the road, then try and figure out which way the killer would have gone – see if anything occurs to me."

"OK. What do you want me to do?" Fahy said.

"Just stay close. I'll tell you what to do when we get going," Lyons said.

The two detectives parked up near the entrance to the estate of houses and got out of the car. They walked together in silence around the entrance to the estate, observing their surroundings carefully. When they got back to the road, Lyons spoke out loud, more to herself than to Sally Fahy.

"Let's see. I've just murdered a woman, so I want to get away from the scene as quickly as possible in case anyone comes along. Which way do I turn – back towards Galway, or on towards Clifden?"

"Galway," Fahy said.

"Yes, I agree. Come on, let's go," Lyons said, indicating that they should turn to the right.

"You go that side, and I'll stay on this side. Look carefully in the verge beside the road, and in the hedge. See if we can find anything that might have been thrown out of the killer's car."

The two detectives walked slowly along the roadside scrutinising the long grass and small ditch at the edge of the road. After almost a kilometre, they had found nothing, and Lyons was getting quite fed up.

"Let the scene speak to me indeed, Mick. You have to be joking!" she said to herself in frustration.

She shouted across the road to Fahy, "Come on, let's go, this is a waste of time."

The two walked back to their car.

"We'd better stop at the garage up the road and get some fuel. It's funny, when the garage sold me the new car, they didn't tell me I'd have to put petrol in it!" Lyons said.

They pulled onto the forecourt of the filling station which had a large convenience store attached that sold everything from bales of peat for the fire to headache tablets, and of course a wide range of teas, coffees and soft drinks.

As Lyons started filling the car from the pump, Fahy said, "Fancy a coffee, boss?"

"Yes, please. Two sugars, and see if they have a sambo or something, I'm starving."

As Fahy entered the shop, she noticed a sheet of paper torn from a spiral notebook stuck to the inside of the glass door with black writing scrawled on it, "Set of keys found – ask inside".

While she ordered the coffees and browsed the sandwiches, a thought occurred to her.

At the cash desk, she paid for the refreshments and produced her warrant card.

"I'd like to see the keys that were handed in, please," she said to the girl behind the till.

"Hold on a minute, I think Martin has them. He's out the back," the girl said, and then disappeared through a grey door. A moment later she was back, clutching a small set of keys comprised of two Yale door keys, a brass Chubb key and a Ford car key with fob.

Fahy was joined by Lyons who came in to pay, having filled her car.

"What have you there?" she said to Fahy.

"I asked them for the keys that were handed in. I thought we might try them up at number twenty-two, just in case."

"Hmm, good idea."

Chapter Five

"Mr McCutcheon, this is Detective Inspector Flynn here from Galway. I was wondering if you'd have a few minutes? There's just something we need to check."

"Well, it's pretty busy here just now, but if you can make it quick," McCutcheon said.

"Thanks. Yes, it's about the other night when you said you went out for a couple of hours. I need to know exactly where you were, and if anyone can corroborate it," Flynn said.

"What! Surely you don't think I had anything to do with that poor woman's death, do you?"

"If you could just tell me where you were, Mr McCutcheon, I'm sure we can clear this up very quickly," Flynn said. He was sorry now that he had decided to do this over the phone. It was so much better to eyeball a witness when asking awkward questions. They gave so much away with their body language.

"I'm sorry, Inspector, I can't tell you. All I will say is that it was a perfectly innocent few hours, and I wasn't anywhere near Owen Glen, and I had nothing whatsoever to do with the death of that woman. Now, if you don't mind, I need to get on," McCutcheon said.

"I'm sorry, Mr McCutcheon, I really have to insist."

"Insist all you like, I'm not saying any more. Now I have to go. Goodbye, Inspector."

Flynn put down the phone, and paused to collect his thoughts. "Damn," he thought, "I should have gone out there."

* * *

Lyons and Fahy made their way back to number twenty-two Owen Glen. Fahy tried the keys in the door of the cottage, and to her surprise, the door yielded immediately to the second Yale key on the keyring.

"Excellent, Sally. Well done. Now all we have to do is find out who they belong to," Lyons said.

"Well, let's take them back to Sinéad and see if she can get any prints off them. Maybe she'll be able to trace the car key as well. Here's hoping," Fahy said.

The two detectives set off down to the entrance to the estate, and as they walked back towards the main road, Fahy was unconsciously pressing the button on the key fob. As they passed number twelve, the four orange indicator lights on a Ford Fiesta parked outside the house flashed, and there was a noisy clunk as the car door locks popped open.

"Was that you?" Lyons asked.

"Yes, I think it was. I was just pressing the button on the key fob. That's interesting – I wonder who lives here?" Lyons said.

"I think I remember. When we were out talking to the McCutcheons, they said that there was a woman who did a bit of cleaning for them that lived at number twelve, but I can't remember her name. Let's knock and find out," Fahy said.

Fahy knocked on the bright green door of number twelve, and a moment later the door was opened by a small thin woman in her late fifties with short grey curly hair, wearing an apron.

"Yes," she said as she looked somewhat bewildered at the two detectives.

Fahy introduced them and showed the woman her warrant card, saying, "And you are?"

"Agnes, Agnes Greely. How can I help you?" the woman said a little nervously.

"Mrs Greely, may I ask if you have the keys to your car handy?" Lyons said.

Agnes Greely said nothing, but went inside the house, reappearing a moment later with a single Ford key with a small white cardboard label attached to it by a piece of cotton thread. Lyons could read the word 'spare' written in blue ink on the paper label.

"Thank you. This is your spare key. May I ask where the other one is?" Lyons asked.

"I don't know where it is, I've mislaid it, but it will turn up. I'm always losing stuff these days," the woman said wringing her hands, which Lyons noticed were badly gnarled with arthritis.

"Would this be it?" Fahy said, holding up the little bunch of keys that they had been given at the petrol station. The woman looked quizzically at the contents of Fahy's open palm.

"God, I'd say that's them, all right. Where did you get them?" Mrs Greely said.

"They were handed in at the petrol station. Someone found them at the side of the road. Mrs Greely, may we come in, please? We need to ask you a few questions," Lyons said.

Agnes Greely instinctively turned to look back inside the little house, before saying to Lyons, "Well, I suppose so. It's not very tidy just now, I have just started cleaning up." She stood back to allow Lyons and Fahy into the small reception room that doubled as a kitchen.

"Can I get you a cup of tea?" Agnes said as they sat down on the two-seater sofa.

"No, we're fine, thanks. We won't keep you long," Fahy said.

Agnes Greely sat at one of the three wooden chairs that surrounded the small, bare dining table in the middle of the room.

"Mrs Greely, we think that your keys may have been discarded by someone who had something to do with the murder of the woman up at number twenty-two the other night. Can you tell us who would have had access to those keys, please?" Lyons asked.

Fahy had her notebook out, and was preparing to take down every word the woman said from now on.

Agnes shifted uneasily in her chair, and looked down at the floor.

"I'm a bit short these days, you see. There hasn't been much cleaning work for the last few months, and the pension isn't really enough for me to make ends meet," she said.

"I'm sorry, I don't understand," Lyons said.

"God, this is awful. Will I get into trouble do you think? I'm only just managing as it is," Agnes went on.

"Can you just tell us what's been going on, please, Mrs Greely," Lyons said, starting to become a little impatient with the woman's procrastination.

"I gave the keys to the woman. She only wanted to stay one night, and she paid me fifty euro in cash, poor soul." Agnes said.

"What woman? The woman who was killed?" Lyons said.

"Yes, yes that's her, Maria Geller. She's foreign you know," Agnes said, her eyes welling up with tears at the memory of the visitor.

"Sorry, I don't understand, Agnes, how did you come to let Maria Geller into the cottage?" Lyons said.

"Well, you see, when Mr McCutcheon hasn't any bookings, I sometimes let people in for a night or two myself. It's no harm. I clean up after them right proper, and they don't use much electric. And I need the money," Agnes said, sniffing loudly.

"I see. And I presume Mr McCutcheon knows nothing about this?" Lyons said.

"Sure, of course he doesn't. He'd string me up alive if he knew, but he's never here. He has that fancy shop all the way over in Westport that keeps him busy."

"How did Maria Geller know you to get in touch?" Lyons said.

"She was here a few times before. The first time she booked it regular like, on Airbnb. Then we got talking when I was doing the cleaning up there, and she asked if she could come back once in a while and deal directly with me. She said it was better, as she didn't want all and sundry knowing her business. So I gave her my phone number, and she'd call a few days before she got here to see if the place was available. There was no harm in it, really," Agnes said.

"May I see your mobile phone, please, Mrs Greely?" Fahy said

"What? What mobile phone. I don't have one. It's the old post office telephone for me," the woman said. She pointed to an old black rotary dial telephone on the kitchen work-top – the type with a coiled cable connecting the receiver to the instrument.

"Did Geller come on her own?" Lyons said.

"Oh, yes, always. Always on her own, and she just stayed one or two nights at most."

"Did she have a car?" Lyons said.

"No, she never did. I used to collect her from the bus here in Clifden, and bring her out, and then take her back the next day."

"What about visitors? Did she have anyone regular calling on her?" Lyons said.

"Now, I wouldn't be snooping into anyone's business. I never saw no one calling, but then I wasn't looking for anyone either. What she got up to was her own business," Agnes said indignantly.

"And on the night she was killed, did you see anyone or hear anything out of the ordinary?" Lyons said.

"No. Like I told the other policeman, I think I heard a car leaving the Glen during the night, but I don't know what time it was, and I didn't even see it. I could have been dreaming. Will Mr McCutcheon have to find out?" Agnes said.

"Probably. We need you to come into the Garda station and make a proper statement about all of this, Mrs

Greely. We can take you in now, if that's convenient?" Lyons said.

"God, I suppose so. Get it over with. I've been very foolish."

Despite Mrs Greely's protestations, Lyons insisted that she travelled into Clifden in the back of Lyons' car. She would have preferred to have taken her own car, but Lyons wasn't having it. When they got to the Garda station, Lyons asked Fahy to take Mrs Greely in and get her statement. "I need to have a word with Sergeant Mulholland. I'll catch you a bit later," Lyons said.

Sally Fahy took Agnes Greely into one of the interview rooms and arranged a coffee for both of them while she took her statement.

Lyons found Séan Mulholland in the back office.

"Hi Séan. Listen, could we go out for a few minutes and get a coffee or something?" Lyons said.

Mulholland sensed that there was something up, so he agreed readily. The two made their way into Cusheen's Bar where Mulholland was well known. It was deserted at that time of day, and Mulholland ordered two coffees and sat well away from the bar beside the fireplace.

"What's up, Maureen?" he asked when they were settled.

Lyons explained what she had discovered about Peadar Tobin's part time work as a handyman for McCutcheon's rental houses.

"It wouldn't matter if this thing hadn't come up. I know many of the lads have a bit of extra work to supplement their income. No one minds as long as it doesn't cross over with official business. He's just been a bit unlucky this time," Lyons said.

"You can say that again."

"Did you know he was working for McCutcheon?" Lyons asked.

"Look, Maureen, can you let me deal with this? Peadar is a good lad. He works hard, and he's very obliging. He's well liked in the town as well. It would be a real favour if we could handle this locally. What do you say?" Mulholland said.

"I don't know, Séan. These things have a habit of coming back and biting you in the arse. But I see what you're saying," Lyons said.

"But it will be my arse, if it does go wrong, Maureen. No need for you to be involved at all."

"If only he hadn't been the first responder, it would look much better if there had been two officers at the scene if it does come back at us."

"That's just what I was thinking. Look, leave it with me. I'm sure I can sort it out," Mulholland said.

"Well, if you're sure, Séan. But for fuck sake, keep me out of it. I don't fancy a posting to the Aran Islands at this stage!" Lyons said.

"Don't worry, girl. By the time this mess is all sorted, no one will know a thing about it," the wily old sergeant said, tapping the side of his nose with his forefinger, and smiling.

* * *

When Sally Fahy had finished taking Agnes Greely's statement, they drove her back out to her house at Owen Glen. It was clear that she was very bothered at being caught with her lucrative little side-line, and the Gardaí weren't about to provide any reassurance in that regard. They left her at her house, and travelled back in to Galway through the bright afternoon sunshine. On the way back, Lyons called ahead and arranged a briefing of the team for five o'clock, and asked Mary Costelloe to see if she could get Sinéad Loughran to come across to the meeting as well.

* * *

"Right, folks," Lyons said, standing at the top of the incident room where a whiteboard had been positioned, "let's see what we have so far. We now know the victim's name was Maria Geller, and we believe she's a foreigner, but we don't have any clue about from where as yet. She's been to Clifden before, and stayed in that very house on a few occasions, but the owner was unaware, as she had an arrangement with the cleaner. The cleaner's phone is an old Post Office job that doesn't have a memory that would give us Geller's mobile number. We can assume that she wanted to keep her presence in the house confidential, at least to some extent. Sinéad, have you discovered anything from your examination of the body and the murder weapon?"

"Yes, quite a bit, actually. Firstly, you'll recall she was holding something in her clenched fist when we found her. That turned out to be a small solid gold ingot," Loughran said, holding up a plastic evidence bag with the shiny yellow metal clearly visible. "There's only the victim's prints on it, and we haven't traced the origin of the gold yet, so that might tell us something when we do."

"Take it down to our good friends in Hartman's. They've been helpful with this kind of thing in the past," Lyons said.

"Good idea. I'll send Deirdre Mac down with it in the morning. As you know, we examined the woman's clothes too. At first we thought they were just standard M&S stuff, but we took a note of the style numbers from the labels and called their head office in Dublin, and they told us that those designs weren't sold in Ireland or the UK. They're doing a bit more rooting around for us to see if they can establish exactly where the items were purchased. We should know tomorrow," Loughran said.

"What about the weapon? Anything there?" Eamon Flynn asked.

"Precious little, I'm afraid. The knife is a bog standard kitchen item, but the green handle is a bit unusual. It may even have been in the cottage all along. We'll be checking with the owner to see if he has an inventory, and if he has, if it's on it. There weren't any useful prints."

"Dr Dodd mentioned that you might be able to get some information from fibre particles left on the woman's neck. Any luck?" Lyons said.

"We're still analysing those. I'll know more tomorrow, but what I can tell you is that it was quite a fine cord with a distinctive criss-cross pattern to it. We didn't find any other trace of it at the scene."

"Thanks, Sinéad. Eamon, did you follow up with McCutcheon?" Lyons said.

"Yes, boss, I did – but I'm afraid I made a bit of a mess of it. I should have gone out there but I called him on the phone instead. I got nothing. He wouldn't say what he was doing that evening, but if he was back home when he said, he can't be our man anyway."

"Still, he's obviously got something to hide. Why don't you get one of the boys from Westport to pay him a visit at the shop and lean on him a bit? We can't just leave that hanging," Lyons said.

"Will do," Flynn said.

"Inspector, why do you think the killer took the keys and dumped them on the road?" Mary Costelloe said.

"Good point, Mary. Maybe he or she was planning on returning to the property, and in the heat of the moment didn't realise he'd left the door open, or perhaps thought that the place would be locked up when he returned."

"Yes, but why would he throw them away then? It doesn't make sense to me," Costelloe said.

"I see what you mean. We'll check that out. OK, so now that we have the victim's name, we can start looking into who she was, and what she was doing here. Sally, tomorrow morning will you get onto the immigration people in Dublin airport and see if they have a record of her coming through, where she flew in from and if she was travelling alone? Then get onto the airline and see what you can find out. See if you can get her bank details – get Mary to give you a hand. John, I want you to do a thorough comb out of all the social media sites you can think of using the name Maria Geller, and see if you can get anything," Lyons said. She looked around the room, and decided that it was time to call it a day.

"Right, that's it everyone. Let's reconvene tomorrow at around lunchtime for an update. Thanks."

* * *

Lyons was tidying up her desk, logging off her computer and getting ready to go home when her phone rang.

"Hi, it's me," Superintendent Mick Hays said.

"Hi, Mick. I'm just about to head home. What about you?"

48

"Nah, I have to finish writing up this blasted budget nonsense. Plunkett needs it for the morning. He's heading up to the Park for a meeting early on, so he needs it finished tonight. Listen, could you pop up for a minute?" Hays said.

"Sure, give me two secs."

Lyons made her way up to the top floor of the building where Superintendent Mick Hays had his spacious office. She didn't knock.

"Hi. Come in. Grab a seat," Hays said.

"Thanks. What's up?" Lyons said.

"Plunkett wants an update on the dead woman out at Owen Glen. He thinks he might get questioned about it up in Dublin, so he wants to be prepared. What's the position?"

"There isn't a position, Mick." She told him all that they knew about Maria Geller and her killer, which didn't amount to very much.

"Hmm, I see what you mean. That's not going to keep Plunkett happy. Any positive lines of enquiry at all?" Hays asked.

"Well, it is early days," she said rather defensively, "and we're doing all the usual stuff. Any advice for me?"

"I'm sure you're doing fine without my interference. But since you ask, I'd say follow the money. That's what I've done in the past when I'm stuck, and it usually helps to shake things up enough to produce a few leads," Hays said.

"OK, but there isn't really a money trail to follow. Unless I'm missing something," Lyons said.

"Get onto Airbnb. Their headquarters is in Dublin now. Get them to trace the first time she booked the

49

cottage on their site. That will give you her card details, and you can follow up with her bank, and so on," Hays said.

"God, Mick, that's brilliant. Now I know why I miss you so much on the team," she said, really meaning it.

Hays blew on his fingernails and feigned polishing them on his jacket lapel.

"Oh, it's nothing really – just pure genius!"

"So, how much longer are you going to be with these blasted budgets of yours, Mr Genius?"

"About an hour at most, I'm nearly done. If you fancy hanging around for a while we could go and eat?" he said.

"You're on. Come down when you're finished and we'll head out."

Lyons made her way back down to her own desk. Once again, she felt that Hays had provided the inspiration that she relied on to move the case forward. She didn't like to admit it, but she frequently had doubts about her own abilities as a super sleuth, and Hays had just endorsed that feeling in her – unwittingly of course.

Chapter Six

By morning, Inspector Eamon Flynn had been onto a colleague in Westport and explained the situation with Batty McCutcheon. The Westport man, an Inspector by the name of Gerry McKeever, was a bit uneasy about having to tackle McCutcheon, due to his standing in the community.

"I hear what you're saying, Eamon, but do you not think there could be an innocent explanation? I mean, he's a well-respected businessman here in the town, you know?" McKeever said.

"I'm sure he is, but we need to know where he was that evening, Gerry. And I don't want to have to drive all the way out there again myself this morning, if I can avoid it," Flynn said.

"Right, so. I'll drop in on him during the day and see what he has to say for himself. I'll let you know, Eamon."

"Thanks, Gerry. I owe you one."

* * *

It was late morning when Gerry McKeever called to the Eurosaver shop in the main street of Westport. He found Batty McCutcheon strutting about inside, barking orders at the black-clad girls, who looked terrified.

McKeever caught the big man's eye.

"Could we have a word outside, Mr McCutcheon?" the inspector said.

McCutcheon said nothing, but followed McKeever as he went out of the shop onto the street.

"Thanks, Mr McCutcheon. Listen, I'm sorry to have to ask you, but we need to know where you were the evening the woman was killed out at your cottage in Owen Glen. It's important," the detective said.

"Right. Well, listen now, this is to go no further, do you hear? I was with one of the girls from the shop. Round at her place – just having a chat, if you know what I mean," McCutcheon said, looking down at his shoes.

"I see. And which girl are we talking about here?"

"Ineke, her name is. But I don't want anyone going around bothering her now. And my wife doesn't have to know, does she?"

"Well, I'll have to check this out with the girl. But if she confirms that you were with her, then we should be able to leave it at that, at least as far as I'm concerned. But I should tell you, there's a Senior Inspector in Galway who's inclined to be very thorough, so I'd be a bit careful for a while if I were you," McKeever said.

"Well, Inspector, I'm sure you'll be able to handle that for me. And don't think I won't be very grateful, if you know what I mean," McCutcheon said, looking directly at McKeever.

"Let's leave it at that for now. Where can I find this Ineke?"

McCutcheon told the detective that the girl was working in the shop. He pointed her out to McKeever, and when he asked her, she admitted that she had been with her boss. She was a pretty girl, with short fair hair and bright blue eyes. McKeever couldn't blame the proprietor for being attracted to her, although the girl's motives for getting involved with the boss were not immediately obvious.

* * *

Sinéad Loughran heard back from M&S during the following morning.

"Ms Loughran, this is Celia Butler from M&S in Dublin. You were asking about some of our pyjamas and a dressing gown," the woman said.

"Oh, yes, that's right. Did you manage to find out anything about where they were bought?" Loughran said.

"Yes, I did. It's a bit odd really. Those lines were specially manufactured for our stores in Eastern Europe – you know, Poland, Czech Republic, Lithuania and so on. Most of those shops are closed down now. It didn't really work out for us out there I'm afraid, so the garments must be a couple of years old at least. Is that any help?" Butler said.

"Well, yes, I suppose so. Are you able to say which store, or even which country they came from?" Loughran asked.

"I'm afraid not. The product codes and style numbers aren't that specific. And with the shops closed now, there's not much more we can do."

Then Loughran had an idea.

"I don't suppose there's any chance that the stock was brought back here, or to the UK, when the Eastern European shops closed down, and sold a bit nearer to home?"

"Oh, no. Definitely not. We don't operate like that. The stock would have been disposed of locally through discount chains once the stores had been closed. I'm sorry I can't tell you more," Butler said.

"Oh, no, that's fine, thanks. You've been very helpful."

* * *

Deirdre Mac arrived in Hartman's jewellers during a lull in trade halfway through the morning. The ever-helpful Monika was cleaning the glass topped counter with a bright green cloth, and put it aside when Deirdre came in.

"Hi. I'm Deirdre MacAllister from the Garda forensic unit here in Galway. I was wondering if you could help us with this," she said, producing the small plastic evidence bag with the little gold ingot in it.

"May I see?" Monika said, extending a hand across the counter.

Deirdre handed it over.

"May I take it out of the bag?" Monika said.

"Yes, of course."

The girl eased open the bag and removed the gold bar, turning it over in her hand. Then she took a loupe from a shelf beneath the counter, put it to her eye, and examined the item closely.

"Well," she said removing the loupe, "it's definitely gold. Very pure too, but it's not local. There is a smelter's mark, but it's very indistinct. I'd say it was possibly Russian, or Eastern European at least. You can buy these on the internet these days, you know."

"Have you seen any of these around here at all recently?" Deirdre asked.

"No. We have quite a few customers who buy gold in this form. Usually bigger 250 gram or 500 gram bars. But of course ours come from fully authenticated suppliers in the UK or Germany, complete with documentation," Monika said.

"Really? It's a popular product then?"

"Very. Ever since the financial crash, people don't trust banks at all. You'd be surprised how many customers have a little stash of gold in their house. Mind you, it's not always in bars – lots of people just buy rings, or bracelets. But the gold ingots are better value. There's no craftsman's costs added on."

"What's this one worth then?" Deirdre asked.

Monika reached below the counter and lifted up a small electronic scale. She placed the gold on the scales, looked at the reading, and then reached for a calculator.

"There's 20 grams here, and at today's price, that's just a little over 700 euro," Monika said.

"Wow, expensive stuff, this gold."

"The price fluctuates almost daily, but not by a lot. It's been rising steadily now for a few years."

"Well, thanks for your help. I'd better take it back and put it away safely. I had no idea it was worth that much," Deirdre said.

* * *

Sally Fahy was having a tough time with Airbnb. Even getting a phone number to call them had been a challenge, and when she did get through, it was to a humble agent who had no authority to say or do anything much. The agent offered to get someone more senior to call Sally back, but she declined the offer, preferring to hold on whilst the wheels moved ever so slowly to get her further up the food chain.

After about forty minutes, most of which was spent listening to dreadful music, she got to speak to Blanad McGonigle, who described herself as a Senior Customer Care Manager. Fahy wasn't too inspired by the woman's name, but she persisted nevertheless, asking about the records of the firm's lettings at 22 Owen Glen to Maria Geller.

"We have to be so careful these days, you know, what with the new data protection regulations and so on. We can get into terrible trouble for disclosing information about our customers," McGonigle said.

"Yes, I'm sure," Fahy said, losing patience after such an interminable wait to speak to someone who could actually help, "but I'd prefer not to have to get a warrant if it can be avoided," she said.

McGonigle said nothing, but Fahy could hear the clack clack of the woman's keyboard, so she assumed that she was continuing with the enquiry.

"Yes, here we are. Ms Geller booked the house on two occasions through us. The first time was in September last year, then again in November. Nothing since. Each booking was for two nights. Odd that. Most of Mr McCutcheon's bookings are for a week at a time. Anyway, what else did you want to know?" McGonigle said.

Fahy asked for the exact dates, and Geller's home address as well as details of the method of payment that had been used. McGonigle parted with the information, still somewhat reluctantly, but handed it over all the same.

When the call was finished, Sally Fahy launched Google Earth on her PC and put in the address that she had been given, which was in Utrecht in the Netherlands. The program searched around aimlessly for a few seconds, and then finally came up with a different address that looked a bit like the one it had been given, but was not the same. Fahy checked it again, just to be certain that she hadn't typed it in wrongly – but she hadn't. It looked as if Maria Geller had been lying about where she lived.

Conscious that Lyons had asked her to get in touch with immigration at Dublin airport, Fahy handed the details over to Mary Costelloe and told her to get John O'Connor's help and pursue enquiries about the credit card that Geller had used.

Now armed with three dates that she knew Maria Geller had been in Ireland, Fahy contacted her colleagues in immigration at Dublin airport. She got speaking to an Inspector Dillon, who hailed originally from Galway, and was only too pleased to help.

Fahy gave Dillon the dates that Geller had been renting 22 Owen Glen, and Dillon got busy looking her up on his system. These days, everyone who comes through Dublin Airport has their passport scanned, so although the numbers are substantial, an efficient database system allows immigration officers to track people's movements relatively quickly for just this type of enquiry.

"Yes, here we are. Maria Geller. She was travelling on a Dutch passport, and she came into Dublin on each occasion from Schiphol," Dillon said.

"Schiphol – that's Amsterdam, isn't it?" Fahy asked.

"Yes, sorry, that's right. There are no notes on the file here about her. She just looks like an ordinary visitor as far as we are concerned. Why the interest?" Dillon said.

Fahy explained that the woman had been brutally murdered in very mysterious circumstances out in Connemara.

"God, that's awful. I guess we won't be seeing her through here again then," Dillon said.

"Well, maybe just once. But she'll be in a wooden box if we can find out exactly where she came from. We have no address for her as yet," Fahy said.

"Oh? I just might be able to help you out there, Sergeant. We're on very good terms with the Dutch immigration lads and lassies in Amsterdam. There's lots of comings and goings we share with them, and I've got to know some of them pretty well over the past few years. Would you like me to give them a call — see if they have anything on your Maria Geller?" Dillon said.

"God, would you? That would be great — thanks very much," Fahy said.

"Ah, 'tis no bother. Anything for a fellow Galwegian. Give me your number and I'll get back to you," Dillon said.

* * *

Lyons was becoming very frustrated at the lack of progress in the case. While they had a number of threads of enquiry going, nothing had produced anything meaningful so far, and Lyons wasn't the type to just sit and wait for something to happen. She dialled Mick Hays' extension to see if he could provide any inspiration, but he was away from his office at one of his confounded meetings, and wouldn't be back until much later in the day.

Lyons barely managed to stop herself going out into the open plan and harassing the team who were all working on their own pieces of the puzzle.

To keep herself distracted, she logged into the Europol database, and keyed in the name Maria Geller. The system came back with all sorts of questions, such as the woman's date of birth, her maiden name, if any, her address and so on, none of which Lyons had to hand, so she just requested a search on the name alone. The Europol system presented a small spinning egg-timer on the screen that seemed to go on for ever, adding to Lyons' frustration. Eventually, just as Lyons was about to give up on it, the screen filled with a list of five Maria Gellers and an invitation to click on the names to expose further information. Three of the names related to German citizens, one was French, and the last one was from the Netherlands. Lyons went through them one at a time. The first four had various indictments listed briefly against their names, and the name of the appropriate police station to contact if further enquiries were needed. When Lyons got to the last one on the list, there were no crimes recorded, simply a message to contact Inspector Luuk Janssen in Utrecht, but no other details were provided.

Lyons was pondering what to do next, when Sally Fahy knocked at her door.

"Hi, Sally. Any news?" she asked.

Fahy told Lyons about the information she had gleaned from the passport control officer at Dublin Airport, and the fact that the murdered woman had given a false address to the rental company when she was booking her stay at Owen Glen.

"The bloke in passport control rang me back too. He's been in touch with his colleagues in Amsterdam airport, but they said they had no information on Geller," Fahy said.

"Never mind, Sally, at least we can now assume that she is from the Netherlands, and I've found an entry on the Europol database that fits too. Well done you. Do you know if the others have got anywhere tracing the payment details?"

"Sorry, boss. I haven't had a chance to catch up with them yet, I thought you'd want to have this information first."

"Yes, of course, thanks. We can follow that up in a while. Look, can you hang on here a few minutes with me. We have to contact police stations in Utrecht – see if we can locate Inspector Luuk Janssen. Here, you use the desk phone, I'll try my mobile – may as well get some value from my 'free calls to anywhere' plan," Lyons said.

The two detectives placed the calls to the Dutch police stations in Utrecht. They were thankful that the Dutch spoke remarkably good English.

On the third call, Fahy scored a hit.

"Yes, we have Inspector Janssen here. He is assigned to the serious crime unit," the man at the other end said.

"May I speak with him please?" Fahy asked.

"Hold the line," the officer said. Fahy could hear various clicks and beeps as the phone was connected through, and then she heard the unfamiliar long ringtone of the Dutch telephone system. Fahy thought she might have been cut off, and was about to hang up, when a woman answered.

"Kan ik u helpen?" the woman said.

Fahy was unsure how to respond, but quite slowly and deliberately, she asked if she could speak to Inspector Luuk Janssen.

"I'm sorry, he's not here at the moment. Who is calling, please?" the woman said in impeccable English.

Fahy explained who she was and why she was calling, and left her Lyons' number for Janssen to call back, which, she was assured, would be within the day.

"Great, Sally, well done. Now we sit and wait – again!" Lyons said.

Chapter Seven

By late afternoon there had been no word back from Utrecht, and given that the Netherlands operates on Central European time and is therefore an hour later than Galway, Lyons' hopes of hearing from Inspector Janssen were fading.

She called the team together for an update, and told them what they had learned about the dead woman.

"How have you been getting on tracing the money, Mary?" Lyons asked.

"Not very well, I'm afraid. We got onto the company that issued her credit card. It was one of those prepaid cards where you lodge money onto it and then use it like an ordinary Mastercard to pay for things. We tried to find out if she had transferred money onto it from another bank, but it seems she just went into a Western Union office with cash, and did it that way," Mary said.

"Well, they must have posted the card out to Geller's address in the first instance. Did you get that from them at least?" Lyons said.

"Sorry, boss. It was sent to one of those places that allow you to receive post using their address for a small fee, and then it was collected along with some other stuff. We couldn't get any further with that I'm afraid."

"Bloody hell! Look guys, this is turning into a right old mystery. We need to start getting some results here or we're going to look very foolish indeed. Let's leave it for this evening, but tomorrow morning I want a brainstorming session here at nine o'clock. You know the rules – nothing is ruled out, no matter how daft it might seem. We'll put everything up on the whiteboard, unchallenged, and then try to make some sense of whatever we've got. You can think about it overnight. OK?"

A murmur of agreement went around the room, and the team started to break up and head for the door.

Lyons went back into her office to tidy up her papers and log off her computer. She was feeling quite down. This wasn't going well – not well at all. She needed some quality thinking time.

As she was wondering how best to achieve something, Sally Fahy put her head round the door to say good night.

"Are you OK, boss?" she asked, seeing that Lyons was down in the dumps.

"No, not really, Sally. This thing is getting me down. I feel as if we should be doing better. God knows what Mick will say, and the last thing we need is for some sharpshooters from Dublin to be given the case because we can't hack it."

"You need alcohol, Maureen."

"No, I'm OK thanks. I better get off and see if I can figure any of this out before the morning."

"There's a bottle of Pino Grigio with our name on it chilling in Doherty's across the road – I insist!"

"Well, OK then, when you put it like that. Just the one mind, then I'm off," Lyons said.

The two women went across the road to Doherty's. When they were seated in a quiet spot with a generous measure of chilled white wine in front of each of them, Fahy said, "Maureen, you don't want to let this thing get you down. Sure, it's a tough case, but we'll get there. We're a good team, and all we need is a break and it will open right up – you'll see."

"I dunno, Sally. I'm supposed to be inspiring everyone, and I feel totally useless on this one. I can't stand all this hanging around. I much prefer it when there's a bit of action – you know, like that business out in Clifden when the two brothers were doing over the hotel. That's more my style."

"Jesus, Maureen, you're incorrigible! You'd prefer to be shot at than sitting in a nice cosy office tapping your computer keys," Fahy said.

"Well, at least when you're being shot at, something is happening. Mind you, I didn't like that business where I nearly got burnt alive at the airport. That was a bit too close for comfort."

"Listen, we'll get this lot sorted. Don't worry – be patient. And don't worry about the case being taken off you. There isn't anyone else that could do any better, and Mick knows that better than anyone. Just hang in there."

* * *

Lyons was on her way home in the car when her phone rang. She had it connected to the Bluetooth, so she was able to answer without touching the handset.

"Lyons."

"Good afternoon, Inspector. This is Luuk Janssen from Utrecht. I got your number from Sergeant Fahy. Is it a good time to talk?"

Lyons pulled the car into the side of the road.

"Yes, of course, Inspector, thanks for calling back."

"That's not a problem. So, you have an interest in our Maria Geller. What has happened?"

Lyons went on to explain about the murder of the mysterious woman at Owen Glen, and then asked Janssen what interest the Dutch police had in her.

"We have been keeping an eye on Ms Geller for some time. She is, or was, a very clever woman. We believe she's involved with smuggling and VAT avoidance involving precious metals – particularly gold. We have had very little luck in actually getting any real evidence. But now, perhaps this will help us," Janssen said.

"Help you? How can her death help you?"

"We are absolutely certain that the woman wasn't acting alone. There is some kind of gang at work here, and we think she may have been near the top of the chain. Look, Inspector, I don't want to say too much on the telephone. Do you think it would be possible for me to come to Ireland to meet with you and your team to see if we could take this further?"

"Possibly. I'll have to check with management, but it could be helpful. It would just be a courtesy of course, we would retain jurisdiction."

"Yes, yes of course. But this is quite a big operation involving millions of euro worth of VAT and quite a lot of criminal activity, so it would be very nice to crack it open."

"Yes, I agree. Let me speak to our management tomorrow and you do the same on your side. Then I'll call you and we can make the arrangements if it's going ahead. OK?"

"Yes, fine and thanks. I look forward to meeting you," Janssen said.

* * *

Lyons was in the kitchen working on a Jamie Oliver 15-minute recipe when Hays arrived home. He came into the kitchen to where Lyons was standing at the cooker and put his arms around her waist, kissing the back of her head.

"God, Maureen, that smells good," he said, stepping back.

"It's only supposed to take 15 minutes, but I've been prepping the veg and the chicken for at least half an hour already. Are you hungry?" she asked.

Hays smacked her gently on the rear end.

"Not the food, silly. I miss working with you, you know. We've had some fun in amongst all the violence and nonsense. Now it's just endless meetings over things that don't seem to be that important if you ask me," Hays said.

"Well, spare a thought for this poor front-line detective who is faced with an impossible case that she can't crack," Lyons said.

The food was almost ready, and although it had taken longer to prepare than she had hoped, it did smell delicious. Lyons went to the fridge and took out a chilled bottle of Chardonnay and handed it to Hays to open and pour.

"Don't worry, Maureen. It's early days, and if I know you, it won't be long before you have a breakthrough."

Lyons handed him a plateful of the colourful concoction she had been preparing on the stove. Hays sat down at the table and waited for Lyons to join him before starting to eat.

"Mmmm, this is delicious. So, what's happening?" he said, taking his first mouthful.

"Well, we'll see. I have some guy from Utrecht coming over to lend a hand – or get in the way, I'm not sure which. It seems the Dutch police have been taking an interest in our Ms Geller for some time," she said. "Did you brief Plunkett on the case?"

"Oh, yes. He's happy enough, for now. He has every faith in you and the team."

"How did he get on in Dublin?" Maureen asked.

"OK, I think. He didn't say much about it. I think he left the file with them. There's plenty going on up there at the moment. I doubt if they have much time to spend bothering us, to be honest. But you never know."

* * *

Mick Hays and Maureen Lyons rose the following morning at 7:30 as usual. After consecutive showers they had a quick cooked breakfast, and drove into the centre of the city. The morning sun was shining on the Atlantic Ocean as they wound their way along the coast through Salthill, and with very little wind, the sea was still and glassy. Offshore, a few boats sat still in the water, punctuating the view of the distant horizon. But neither Hays nor Lyons were concentrating on their surroundings. They were both in their own minds organising their thoughts for the day ahead.

"What have you got on today?" Maureen asked.

"There's a community meeting in the leisure centre at 11. Apparently, there's concern about the number of house burglaries in and around the city, and the usual agitators have been stirring up the good citizens. Then in the afternoon we have a first responders seminar involving the ambulance and fire guys, as well as our own uniformed teams to see if we can co-ordinate things a bit better and try and cut down the time it takes to get to a scene in response to 999 calls," Hays said.

"Nice. Have you anything to offer them – the agitators, I mean?"

"Oh, you know, the usual platitudes – increased patrols around the most vulnerable areas, greater focus on house thefts by the Detective Unit – all the usual bullshit. I was wondering about giving some of it back to them, telling them to get proper alarms fitted to their properties with 24-hour monitoring, that sort of thing. But sometimes that can backfire. I imagine the press will be there, and they'd just love to print a story about the Gardaí abdicating responsibility for crime in Galway and telling citizens to fix it themselves."

"It's not altogether easy, is it? Anyway, our clear up rates are pretty good in that department. If the bloody judges wouldn't insist on putting the little scrotes back out on the street on bail, we'd have a lot less of it," Lyons said.

"What about you? What have you lined up for the day?" Hays asked.

"Well, I'd better see about getting this Dutch guy over. He could actually be helpful. To be honest, I don't know what else we can do for now. I have the team trying to chase down the money, like you suggested, but it's mostly dead ends so far. We need to get lucky," Lyons said.

"Well, you know what they say – 'the harder you work, the luckier you get'."

"Yeah – right!"

Chapter Eight

The team were all gathered in the open plan at five to nine
for the brainstorming session that Lyons had set up the
previous evening. At the top of the room, the whiteboard
carried a photograph of the dead woman, with red lines
linking her picture to Agnes Greely and Batty
McCutcheon. In other boxes on the board, Airbnb and
The Netherlands were inscribed with question marks
against them.

A flip chart stand had been placed alongside the
whiteboard with a pad of paper on it, and an array of
coloured markers in the pen tray.

Lyons stood at the top of the room beside all the
equipment, and addressed the group.

"Right, folks. You know the drill. We'll go around the
room one at a time. Anything – anything at all that you
think could be useful, spit it out, and I'll jot it down here.
No one is allowed to challenge until we've all had a go.
Then we'll go back over everything and rule out the
impossible. As someone once said, 'when you eliminate

the impossible, then whatever is left, however improbable, is the solution to the case'."

A murmur went around the room.

"Let's start with you, Eamon," she said looking at Inspector Eamon Flynn.

Flynn cleared his throat.

"Right. Well, firstly, why were the house keys discarded at the roadside?" he said. Lyons wrote 'Discarded keys' on the flip chart.

"Good one, Eamon," she said.

"And, why was she strangled post-mortem – that's just weird," he went on.

Lyons wrote 'strangled post-mortem' on the board.

"OK. Anything else?" Lyons asked.

"No, that's it," Flynn replied.

"Right. Sally – you're next."

Sally Fahy shuffled a little in her seat.

"I've written down here that we didn't find a phone belonging to the victim. She must have had one, but there was no sign of it anywhere," Fahy said, a little unsure of herself.

"Good point, Sally," Lyons said. She wrote 'victim had no phone' on the flip chart.

"Anything else?" Lyons asked.

"Yes. I have a note here about the gold ingot. Where is it from and why was she holding it? If robbery was the motive, why didn't the thief take that too," Fahy said.

Lyons wrote 'gold ingot in victim's clutch' on the flip chart.

"Thanks, Sally; now Mary, what have you got for us?" Lyons said.

"Liam and I have joined forces on this, if that's OK, inspector?" Mary Costelloe said.

"Yes, sure, that's not a problem. Just tell us what you've got," Lyons said.

"Well, we were wondering if Batty McCutcheon could be involved in some way. He brings all that rubbish he sells in from China after all," the junior officer said.

"Good point, Mary," Lyons responded. She wrote 'McCutcheon – China' on the chart.

"Then we thought about what exactly Maria Geller was doing here in the west of Ireland for just one or two days, three times in a year. What was the purpose of her visit?" she said.

Lyons wrote 'Geller – purpose of visit' on the pad.

"That's it, I'm afraid," Costelloe said.

"OK. Thanks everyone, I'm going to add my five-pence worth now. There's the money. What about the money? Why all the secrecy? And then there's the link to the Netherlands. We'll know more about that when Janssen gets here," Lyons said. She wrote those two things up alongside the rest of the brainstorming output that almost filled two entire pages at this stage.

When they had finished emptying their collective minds, a discussion followed during which the items were each given a score on a scale of one to five, with five being the most important. Lyons then handed out tasks for the team to pursue.

"Eamon. I'd like you and Mary to get to work on McCutcheon. Do it discreetly, but find out everything you can about his business operations. See if there's anything dodgy there – you know, VAT avoidance; skimming cash

– whatever you can get. But I don't want him alerted to what you're doing. Clear?"

"Yes, boss, crystal," Flynn replied.

"Liam, can you work with John O'Connor on the phone? Sally is right – she must have had one. Agnes Greely told us that she called her a couple of times from abroad, and presumably when she arrived at the bus station in Clifden to arrange her lift. So where is it? Who has it?" Lyons said.

"Sally, as soon as I have sorted out this Dutch policeman, you and I are going back out there. The site has more to tell – I can feel it. And if anyone gets anything during the day, I want to know immediately. We'll meet back at five if nothing breaks, and please God we'll have some news. Right, off you go," Lyons said.

As the room cleared, Fahy took down the two pages of bullet points from the flip chart, rolled them up and handed them to Lyons.

"Thanks, Sally. Give me half an hour, then we'll be ready for off. OK?"

"Sure. Fancy a coffee?" Fahy asked.

"Good idea. Mines a latte," Lyons said, and handed Fahy a five euro note.

* * *

When Lyons got back to her office, there was a note on her desk to call Hays. She checked the time, and reckoned he wouldn't have set off yet for the leisure centre. He answered the phone on the first ring.

"Hi. Thanks for calling back. Look, Plunkett wants to see us both, and he didn't sound too cheerful," Hays said.

"Oh. OK. When?"

"Now, if you can manage it," Hays said.

"Sure, see you up there."

Lyons checked her appearance in the mirror she kept in her desk drawer. "You'll have to do, girl," she said to herself, being reasonably happy with her reflected image.

* * *

"Come in, Superintendent, Inspector. Take a seat," Plunkett said from behind his spacious mahogany desk.

"Can I get you a coffee, I'm just about to have one?" he asked.

"No thanks, sir, we're fine," Hays answered for both of them, though in truth, he would have loved a cup.

"As you know, I was up in the Park earlier in the week. The subject of this murder out in Clifden came up. There are some who are a bit unsettled by all the serious crime that's been occurring out in Connemara over the past few years, and they are starting to ask questions of us, if you get my drift," Chief Superintendent Finbarr Plunkett said.

Before either Hays or Lyons could respond, the chief went on, "They're after asking one of their many civilian lads to have a look at our case files going back a bit. So we'll have to be on our toes, and needless to say we need a quick result in this latest caper."

Plunkett looked at them both, clearly expecting some kind of response.

"Yes, sir. I understand what you're saying. But it's very early days on this particular case. And it's not an easy one. Inspector Lyons here is getting on with it, and we're enlisting the help of the Dutch police too. I expect we'll have some news quite shortly," Hays said.

Lyons wasn't at all happy that Hays was speaking on her behalf, but she decided to bite her tongue for the moment. She could deal with that later.

"Good man, Mick, that's what I was hoping you would say. Look, I can hold them off for another few days at least. The good thing about the Park is that things don't move too quickly up there. But I've given some undertakings about the team here in Galway, and I need to demonstrate that it wasn't all hot air. Some of that lot seem to think we're getting a bit too big for our boots, and we need to be knocked back – and that wouldn't suit me at all. Now – do you need any more support or more men or anything from me?" he said, addressing Lyons for the first time.

"No, thank you, sir. As Superintendent Hays says, it's early days, but we are making progress," Lyons said. She decided that this wouldn't be the time to raise the issue that her team was still short of a detective sergeant, as that would probably not reflect well on her partner. But she was peppering nevertheless.

You always knew when a meeting with the chief was over. He looked down at the top of his desk, and managed to find a sheet of paper to study and fondle, so the two thanked him and got up to leave. Plunkett said nothing as they exited into the corridor.

"Jesus, Mick. That man is such a chauvinist! He barely acknowledged my presence at all, and then he was so condescending. I could barely hold my tongue!" Lyons said.

"Easy, tiger. We don't know what sort of shit he has to deal with from above – but it can't be easy. Let's just direct our energy into solving the case. That's the best way to get the upper hand with Plunkett," Hays said.

"And by the way, you owe me a detective sergeant, don't forget!" she said.

"I'm working on it – bloody hell – go easy, will you?"

"It's OK, sir, you just go off to your little group of happy clappies at the leisure centre – I'll get back out there and solve the case, shorthanded and all as we are." With that, Lyons stomped off to her own office leaving Hays bemused in the corridor.

Back in her office, Fahy was waiting with the coffee she had gone out to get earlier.

"Damn it! I could swing for that man sometimes," Lyons said.

"Which one?" Fahy responded.

"Plunkett, of course. He can be such a prick at times."

"No comment," Fahy said, and they both started laughing.

* * *

Lyons had cooled down by the time she and Sally Fahy were driving out to Clifden. It was a lovely, still late spring day, and the bright yellow gorse was just beginning to bloom along the sides of the road out beyond Oughterard. Occasionally, the heady scent of coconut that was given off by the young blooms could be sensed, and the blue of the distant mountains contrasted magically with the early green sprouts of the grasses on the heathland.

"I'd better call Mick and apologise. I was very rude to him, and it was Plunkett I was angry with. You close your ears, I'll call him on the mobile," Lyons said.

She got through to Hays who was just finishing up at the leisure centre.

"Hi. It's me. Look, I'm sorry about earlier. I didn't mean to be rude to you. It's just that man really winds me up sometimes," she said.

"Ah, don't worry. You're right – he can be very annoying. But it's usually when he's under pressure. Don't let it get to you."

"But I shouldn't take it out on you – sorry."

"That's fine, don't worry about it. And by the way, I am working on your extra sergeant. I've been looking for a bloke to put in there, but all I keep getting is highly talented and very pretty young female officers. It's not great for the gender balance."

"You just don't want us to have another hunky young Garda to fight over on the team. I have Sally here in the car beside me, and she's already thinking about a transfer to some all-male unit in the force!"

"Well, I'll see what I can do, but you may have to settle for yet another female. I'll talk to you later about it."

"OK. Thanks, Mick. See ya later, and I'm sorry again for losing it with you," Lyons said.

"All forgotten. See ya."

"God, you two are so good together. How do you manage it?" Fahy said when Lyons had finished the call.

"I know – it's mad. It really should be a disaster, but somehow it works really well for both of us. We spar a bit occasionally – but that's just me – I can be a cranky bitch at times."

"Hmmm, I'm saying nothing, boss."

"So, what would you think about another woman joining us?" Lyons said.

"Doesn't bother me as long as she's good at her job. To be honest, I'd nearly prefer it. Another bloke full of testosterone would only be a distraction, and office romances definitely don't work for me."

"Oh, so you've tried it then?" Lyons said.

"Not really. The occasional fumble after a night out is all – didn't amount to anything, and I wouldn't want it to."

"And who, might I ask, was your fellow fumbler?" Lyons said smiling.

"That's classified information, boss, sorry."

"Hmmm – well, I could guess, but maybe I'd better not. Look, we're just here," she said as they turned into Owen Glen and parked the car on the grass verge.

Chapter Nine

Sally Fahy walked down to the garage where the keys to number 22, along with Agnes Greely's car key, had been handed in. She found Martin stacking the shelves with new stock.

After she had introduced herself, she asked about the person who handed in the keys.

"Oh, right. That was Dinny McHugh, the postman. He said he just found them at the side of the road so he brought them here," Martin said.

"Can you remember what time this was?" Fahy said.

"It was just as we were opening up at nine. Dinny cycles out this far with the post every day. Anything further out is delivered in the van, but he comes out as far as the Glen on his bike, unless the weather is awful. He usually has a cup of tea with us before heading back into town."

"Thanks. That's useful. I think I'll go into Clifden and see if he's still around. Thanks again."

Fahy walked back to where Lyons appeared to be just standing around, but she knew better than to challenge her boss. Lyons' instinct for detection in these situations was legendry. She had been instrumental in solving some of the team's trickiest cases just by soaking up the atmosphere near the location of a crime scene and waiting for inspiration.

After a few minutes, she spoke to her colleague.

"Well, anything?"

Fahy explained that she wanted to go into town and seek out Dinny the postman to ask him about the keys, so Lyons told her to take the car.

"I'll wait for you here, Sally. But don't be too long, and it would be great if you could bring me back a coffee," Lyons said handing over the keys of her car.

"Sure, no worries. See you shortly," Fahy said.

When Sally Fahy had left in Lyons' car, Lyons walked all around the house where Maria Geller had lost her life so brutally. The property was still cordoned off with blue and white crime scene tape, and the front door had been crudely shored up with a batten across the front to deter anyone from getting in. As she turned the corner to walk along the back of the property, she saw that the kitchen window was open, and blowing gently in the breeze. This wasn't right. The last time she had been in the house, the back windows were all closed. Lyons walked over to the window and saw that the glass was broken.

Lyons wasn't tall enough to see right into the house, but standing on tip-toes and holding onto the window frame with her gloved hand, she could see that the glass from the window was scattered on the worktop and the floor, so the window had been smashed from outside. She looked around for something she could stand on to enable her to see in properly. At the back of the next-door property, there was a discarded plastic bottle crate. She went and retrieved it, and placing it underneath the kitchen window of number 22, she stood rather unsteadily on it, and looked in. The kitchen was a terrible mess. Everything had been pulled out of the cupboards and drawers and lay strewn all around. The oven stood open, with the trays and racks pulled out, and the fridge was similarly left open, with the motor purring away in a vain attempt to keep it to the desired four degrees. From her vantage point standing on the crate, Lyons could see that the rest of the house was a mess too. Upturned furniture and cushions were thrown every which way on the floor, and books and magazines joined in to create a chaotic scene.

Lyons got on the phone at once to Sinéad Loughran, team leader of the forensic unit attached to the Galway Detective Unit.

"Hi Sinéad, it's Maureen. I'm out here at Owen Glen. The house has been broken into, and it's been done over. I need you to come out with a few of your guys to do a thorough inspection of the place, see if we can get any prints or other evidence that might tell us who did this and why. Can you drop everything right now?"

"Hi, Maureen. Yes, that's not a problem. Give me forty-five minutes and I'll be with you. I'll bring two of the guys with me as well. Don't go in, will you, unless you already have?" Loughran said.

"No, that's OK. I'll wait outside till you get here."

As Lyons finished the call to Galway, Sally Fahy arrived back having had a brief chat with Dinny the postman.

Lyons explained what she had discovered and said that the forensic team were on their way out.

"What did the postman have to say?" she asked her colleague.

"He says he just found the keys at the side of the road when he was out delivering mail to Owen Glen. It was quite early, and there was no traffic around at all. He says he didn't find anything else – just the keys," Fahy said.

"Damn. This case is really getting me down, Sally. God knows what will happen next. Let's sit in the car and wait for Sinéad."

* * *

Loughran had obviously put the boot down on the drive out from the city. It seemed no time at all before her big white 4x4 was pulling up beside Lyons' new Volvo outside number 22.

"Hi, Sinéad. That was quick," Lyons greeted the girl as they all got out of their vehicles.

"Hi, Maureen, Sally. So, what's the story?" Loughran said as she clambered into her white scene of crime suit.

Lyons explained what she had found at the back of the house.

"OK. Well, we'll need a shoe print from your shoes to eliminate them, and best if you stay clear of the house till I put down some of these yellow plates for us all to walk on," Loughran said, in a business-like tone.

"Fine," Lyons replied.

One of the other members of the forensic team came across to Lyons and asked her to tread on a rectangular pad that would capture an imprint of her shoes. Another member of the team was placing bright yellow plastic 'stepping stones' leading up to the front door, and all around the cottage to the back where the broken window was located.

The team made short work of getting into the house through the front, and then they disappeared inside. As Loughran entered, she turned to Lyons and said, "I'll give you a shout when it's clear to come in. We just need a few minutes to see what we can find first."

"Fine, that's grand," Lyons said, feeling rather surplus to requirements, and she and Fahy sat back into the Volvo.

"Sally, can you knock on a few doors – see if anyone's home, and if they heard or saw anything, anything at all while this was going on. I'll give Séan Mulholland a call and see if he knows anything."

Fahy went off around the neighbouring houses knocking on doors, but very few of the properties were occupied, and even those that exhibited some signs of inhabitancy were deserted. Presumably the people staying there were taking advantage of the good weather to do day trips or go into Clifden for a mooch around.

Lyons' call to Sergeant Séan Mulholland proved to be equally fruitless.

"We've no record of anything out there since the murder, Maureen. Do you want me to send a man out to ye?" he asked.

"Nah. It's a bit late for that, Séan. It's been rightly done over. Was anyone supposed to be keeping an eye on it?"

"No, we weren't. Sure, wasn't the place empty after the poor woman was taken away? We just saw to it that it was closed up properly, and left it at that."

"Well, someone obviously thought it was worth breaking into. We'll let you know when we're leaving, and then maybe you should send a man out to make sure it's secured properly. It would be no harm to send a patrol car around the estate a few times at night too, if you have the resources, Seán."

"Right. I'll arrange that so. Talk to you later."

Loughran appeared at the door and beckoned Lyons into the house. Being careful to step on the yellow slabs that had been put down, Lyons made her way into the hall, and down to the kitchen where Loughran was now bent down, picking up packets and tins of food from the floor. Another member of the team was busy dusting the broken window frame, and Lyons noticed that the door jambs were now covered in the light grey powder that the forensic team used to detect finger and palm prints.

As Loughran picked up a box of cornflakes, she said, "That's odd – this is much heavier than it should be."

She looked inside the box, and slowly withdrew the half-full opaque plastic bag that had been scrunched up to keep the cornflakes fresh. She put the cereal down beside her on the floor and stood up.

"Wow! Have a look at this!"

Lyons was now fully attentive, and stood beside Sinéad Loughran as they both peered into the cardboard container. In the bottom of the box, they could clearly see a collection of gold objects shining up at them.

"Nice one, Sinéad. Gives a whole new meaning to the tag line 'golden flakes of corn', doesn't it?" Lyons said.

Loughran carefully tipped the contents of the box out onto the counter top. There were a number of gold ingots – just like the one that Maria Geller had been clutching in her dead fist when they found her, but a bit bigger – two gold gate bracelets, and a gold chain about half a metre long.

Loughran addressed one of her assistants.

"Shane, could you pop out to the jeep and bring me the scales? You'll find it in the compartment under the front passenger's seat. Thanks."

"Right, boss," the man said.

He was back a minute later with a small electronic scale which Loughran used to weight the gold.

"Crickey! There's almost a kilo here. I wonder what that's worth?" Loughran said.

"Well, it's about €40 a gram, so that lot must be close to €40,000 give or take. But how the hell did whoever broke in not find it?" Lyons said.

"That's easy. Hidden in plain sight – the oldest trick in the book. I've seen that lots of times before. Anyway, best get this bagged up and back into town. Get a good look at it. There may be some useful trace evidence on it."

"So, you're not going straight to the travel agent for a one-way ticket to South America then?" Lyons quipped.

"Not this week, Maureen. Too much work on!"

* * *

When Lyons got back to the office, there was a message for her to call Luuk Janssen. She placed the call, and discovered that he was already booked on a flight to Dublin later that evening, and would be in Galway before the night was out.

"I was wondering if you could recommend a hotel that is near your police station, Inspector?" the Dutchman said.

"Well, we usually use the Imperial on Eyre Square. It's very central, and close to the railway station too. Would you like me to make a reservation for you?" Lyons asked.

"Ah, yes, I am seeing it here on Google maps. No, thank you. It's fine. My office will book me in. How will I find your police station tomorrow morning?"

"That's no problem. I'll send a car to pick you up at, say, 8:45. Is that OK?" Lyons said.

"Yes, that would be perfect. Thank you. See you then."

When Lyons had finished the call with Luuk Janssen she went out into the open plan and told the rest of the group about the find out in Owen Glen.

"The trouble is, I'm not sure if it gets us any further along. Great that Sinéad located the loot, but it doesn't help to explain Geller's murder, except maybe to provide a motive. But even at that, wouldn't the killer have taken the gold if he could? It doesn't make sense to me. In fact, very little of this case makes any sense. Has anyone else got anything useful?" Lyons said.

John O'Connor spoke.

"This may be something and nothing, boss. I had a browse through the 'for sale' ads on ClassicClassifieds.ie just to see if there were any phones that have been put up in the last few days that might be Geller's. I concentrated on the Galway ads and we found three or four. Mary called them, and one might be a bit promising. It was a foreign bloke, and he sounded a bit shifty. He had a laptop for sale too, but didn't seem to know much about it although he said it was his," O'Connor said.

"Sounds promising. What's he looking for the phone?"

"He's asking €300, but I'm sure we could beat him down a bit. Shall I get Mary to try and buy it?"

"Yes, OK. But try and arrange for Mary to collect it at his address, and get her to take Liam along too. He can pretend to be her boyfriend. Get them to have a good look round when they are there – see what they can observe. This may not be connected, but it's worth a try, and €300 shouldn't break the department's budget. Oh, and good work, John. Let's hope it pans out. Did you get a name?"

"Says he's Matis Vitkus, but that could be made up."

"OK, but I'll look him up on Europol just in case. Let me know how it goes."

Chapter Ten

Janssen was shown into Lyons' office the following morning just after 9 a.m. He was a slim man, probably in his late forties, with a good head of hair going silver in colour and a rugged face. He stood at five foot eleven or thereabouts, and was dressed smartly but casually in navy slacks, a dark blue polo shirt and a tan leather jacket. Lyons noticed that he had good quality black leather shoes. She liked men who wore good shoes.

"Good morning, Inspector," Janssen said, extending his hand for a firm handshake, "it's good to meet you."

"Yes, likewise. Come in, take a seat. May I get you a coffee?"

"No thank you, I have just had an amazing breakfast at the hotel, though to be honest, the coffee was a bit weak. In Utrecht we take triple espresso."

"Well, maybe later. So, what can you tell us about Maria Geller?" Lyons said.

"It's a long and complex story, Inspector, and there are still several pieces of the jigsaw missing, which is one of the reasons why I have come to your beautiful country."

"Would you mind if I brought another officer in to hear whatever you have to say?" Lyons said.

"Of course not, and maybe later we could see about talking to your full team?"

"Yes, well, let's see how it goes. I'll fetch Inspector Eamon Flynn in for now."

Lyons didn't like the idea of Janssen addressing the entire team. He was, after all, just an observer as far as the Gardaí were concerned, and she didn't want him taking over. But neither did she want to put him off telling them everything that he knew about the ill-fated Maria Geller. She summoned Flynn to join them in her office.

When the introductions had been made, Janssen told his story.

"We believe Maria Geller was involved with a criminal gang who appear to be operating out of Eastern Europe – quite possibly Lithuania. And it seems they have connections further east as well, almost certainly into China. It's all based around stolen gold – or maybe it would be more accurate to say recycled stolen gold," Janssen said.

"Sorry, Inspector, I don't understand. Recycled?" Flynn said.

"Yes. I'll explain. Since the near collapse of the banking system in Europe, many people don't trust banks to look after their wealth. And with all the new disclosure regulation, it's very hard for the criminal classes to use institutions any longer. So, gold has become once again a safe haven for citizens and criminals alike, especially where hot money is concerned."

"Yes, I would agree. One of the local jewellers here in Galway has told us that they sell quite a lot of gold in the form of small ingots now. But who has enough 'hot money', as you call it, to buy loads of gold?" Lyons said.

"You would be surprised. Anyone who runs a largely cash business. Owners of public houses and bars; restaurants; shops; night clubs – and even the guy who comes to repair your house, or clean your windows," Janssen said.

"But surely they can't skim enough off the top to buy gold?" Flynn said.

"Last year, we arrested a washing machine repair man in Arnhem who was making €250,000 and only declaring €80,000 for tax. And there are many like this who can't afford to be seen banking large amounts. A lot of the gold is bought over the internet, and this is where it gets interesting. As far as we can tell, when people buy the stuff – which is perfectly fine metal, no issue there – the company that sells the bars is passing the names and addresses of the buyers to criminal gangs. These gangs then steal the gold back from the original purchasers and return it to the sellers at a steep discount, and it is then re-sold," Janssen said.

"But why isn't the theft of the gold reported to us?" Flynn said.

"If it is being bought with hot money, then it can't be reported for obvious reasons, Eamon," Lyons said.

"Exactly. But the thieves need a way to get the gold back to where it came from. So, they are using couriers who act as collection agents. These couriers have to be very clever to get through customs without the stolen gold being discovered. We believe Maria Geller was one such," Janssen said.

"And how exactly does the courier smuggle it out?" Flynn asked.

"As you have seen, gold is very small. Some of the bars are the same size as a battery for a mobile phone. Some others can fit inside a laptop computer, and go undetected as the x-ray machine just thinks they are part of the device. If there is jewellery involved, the courier can simply wear it and say it is her own."

"Do they only use women?" Flynn said.

"Yes, mostly, although it depends on where they are travelling to. In Europe, women attract less suspicion at customs, and it's natural for them to have gold jewellery too."

"So, who is making what money from all of this?" Lyons said.

"Well, the original sale of the gold bars is at market value, with sometimes a slight discount to make the deal attractive. The thieves who steal it back, we think, get about 25% of the true value and the courier gets another 10%. Then organised crime steps in and grabs the rest. It's very profitable for them."

"And can you not just close down their web sites?" Lyons said.

"We have tried, believe me. But they keep the web pages the same and move the hosting around the world every few days. Recently, they have established hosting in Venezuela and Paraguay, and you can imagine that the authorities in these countries are not really interested in following it up."

"Hmmm, but what's to stop the burglars from selling the gold themselves and keeping all of the money?" Flynn said.

"Firstly, the thieves wouldn't know who has gold in their homes, and who has not. So they would be working blind, and could easily get caught by the police. Secondly, if the gang got to hear of it – and they would, because the stolen gold would not end up back at the source – they would simply exterminate those concerned in the most brutal fashion. Which prompts me to ask how Maria Geller was murdered?" Janssen said.

"There was something very odd about her killing. She was stabbed through the chest with a kitchen knife. That almost certainly killed her instantly. But then it appears she was strangled, post-mortem, or so our pathologist has told us. We've never seen anything like that before in these parts," Lyons said.

"That is the trade mark of this particular gang. They do this so that their foot-soldiers will get a clear message, and stay in-line. I'm afraid to say, you may have one or more of these disgusting villains in your midst. Inspector Lyons, do you think it would be possible for me to see the body of the dead woman?" Janssen said.

"Yes, I suppose we could arrange that, but I warn you, it's not a pretty sight."

"I'm sure I have seen worse, but thank you."

"Eamon, can you get someone to take Inspector Janssen over to the mortuary? We'll meet up later, if that's OK with you, inspector?" Lyons said.

"Yes, of course."

When Flynn and Janssen had left her office, Lyons sat quietly for a few minutes organising her thoughts. While all that stuff about couriers and organised crime based in Utrecht was fascinating, her job was to see if she could bring the killer of Maria Geller to justice. And so far, they were nowhere near any kind of result on that front. She realised that with Janssen here, and all that other stuff rattling around in people's heads, it was going to be difficult for everyone to stay focussed. She believed that if they could apprehend a few burglars and help to break up a sophisticated organised crime scam along the way, that would be useful, but she doubted that the Gardaí would get any of the credit for it, and her own superiors might easily think she had lost the run of herself, wasting valuable resources on such flights of fancy. She would have to proceed very carefully on this one.

With that in mind, she called Superintendent Mick Hays.

"Hi, Mick, it's me."

"Hello you, what's up?"

"Just wondering if your superintendentness is free for a bite to eat at lunch? I want to run something past you," Lyons said.

"Oh, I guess I could just about tear myself away to meet up with a pretty junior officer. Where do you want to go?"

"Cheeky! Let's meet at The Brasserie at 12:45. I'll book a table, OK?" she said.

"Yes, fine. I'll have a rolled-up newspaper under my arm in case you don't recognise me!"

"God give me strength!" Lyons said laughing down the phone, "go on – I'll see you there."

Chapter Eleven

Mary Costelloe phoned the number on the ClassicClassifieds website for the second time.

"Ja, Matis."

"Hi. My name is Mary, I was on to you earlier about the iPhone. I'd like to buy it, but I was wondering if you could do a little better on the price? I don't have much money just now," Mary said in her best pleading voice.

"For cash, maybe I'll do €275, OK?" Matis said.

"Oh, thank you, that's good of you. I'll take it. Where can I come to collect it?"

"We meet outside in public place. Four o'clock, café in Williamsgate Centre, upstairs, OK?"

"Yes, yes, OK. I'll have my boyfriend with me. How will you recognise me?" Mary said.

"Don't worry, I find you." With that he was gone.

"OK, so far so good, Liam. Now let's get the cash organised. I think we should get there around three thirty and do some window shopping just in case he's keeping watch. I don't like the fact that he says he can identify us even though he has never met either of us," Costelloe said.

"Good idea. Can you organise the cash? We'll head out at around three," Walsh said.

"Great. See you later."

Getting cash from the force to purchase stolen property was a well proven but cumbersome procedure involving the completion of several forms, each of which had to be countersigned by a senior officer. Below €500, an Inspector would suffice – beyond that, it was upstairs to find a superintendent who would be willing to underwrite the transaction. Then you had to find the desk sergeant who had the keys to the station's safe, and treated the money as if it were his own. The cash would be counted out twice in front of you, and of course it had to be signed for again at this point.

Mary found Eamon Flynn at his desk and presented him with the completed forms.

"OK, Mary. What's the plan?" he said as he scribbled his signature on the documents.

"We were thinking once we've bought the phone, we could ask him about the laptop that he advertised too. See if we can get back to his place to have a look at it. Then we'd say that we wanted it, but don't have the cash to buy it just then, and arrange to go back tomorrow. That would give forensics time to see if the phone belonged to Geller. What do you think?"

"Excellent. Sounds like a runner, but be sure not to handle the phone too much. It will already have been wiped clean, but there may be traces caught in around the edges, or in the sim card tray, so get it into a sterile evidence bag as soon as you can," Flynn said.

"Yes, OK, boss. Thanks."

* * *

Costelloe and Walsh got to the shopping centre at just after half past three. They wandered around aimlessly looking in the windows of the brightly lit shops, and Mary even managed to drag her colleague and pretend boyfriend into one of the shoe shops for a closer look at some of the merchandise. All the while, they kept a close look out to see that they weren't being observed, using the reflections in the polished glass of the glitzy shops as a cover. But they could detect nothing, and as four o'clock approached, they made their way to the café and sat down on opposite sides of a three-seater table near the door, with Liam Walsh facing outwards.

"Let's hope he arrives on time," Costelloe said. It was warm in the shopping centre, so she removed her jacket and put it on the back of her chair. She was wearing a snug fitting white blouse underneath her coat that went well with her equally well-fitting denim jeans, and as she sat down again, she opened a button at the top of her blouse to show a little more skin.

"So, that's your game," Walsh said, smirking.

"Well, you know what they say, Liam, 'if you've got it, flaunt it'."

They were just starting into their coffee when a man sat down in the third chair at the table. He was quite a short, thin person, with a shaved head and a mean look about his face. He was dressed in a black polo shirt with some sort of logo on the front that neither of the Gardaí recognized, black jeans and black ankle boots. Liam Walsh guessed he was in his late twenties or early thirties, though it was quite hard to tell.

When he was seated at the table between the two Gardaí, he said simply, "Matis."

Mary Costelloe tried to engage the man in conversation.

"Hi Matis. I'm Mary and this is my boyfriend, Liam. Nice to meet you. Would you like a coffee?"

"No coffee. Just phone. Have you brought the cash?"

"Yes, of course. May I see the phone please?" she said.

Matis reached beneath the table and produced an iPhone. Mary wished she could put on vinyl gloves before picking it up, but that was clearly out of the question. Being careful not to handle the device any more than absolutely necessary, she switched it on and waited for the Apple logo to appear, and then disappear again to be replaced by the word, 'Hello'. So far so good.

"Hmm, that looks OK, Matis. It's in good condition. Why are you selling it?" Liam asked.

Matis looked a little confused for a moment, but recovered quickly.

"Upgrade. I have a new phone," he said.

"Ah, nice. Is this one unlocked?" Mary said.

"Yes, of course. I took to Chinese shop. They unlock it. Now can I have money please?" Matis said. He looked around the café nervously, and Mary noticed that his fingernails were bitten down to the quick, and he was fidgeting a lot.

"Oh, yes, sorry. Liam, can you give Matis the cash? Oh, and I think I saw that you had a laptop computer for sale as well. I would be interested in that too, Matis. Mine got stolen."

Liam counted out the €275 that they had agreed on the telephone, and Matis didn't take his eyes off the money as he replied to Mary.

"Yes, I have laptop too. It's €300," Matis said. He reached out and lifted the folded notes off the table and they disappeared quickly into his jeans pocket.

Mary leaned in towards the man as she spoke, giving him a whiff of her perfume and a glimpse of cleavage. "Do you think you could do it a little bit cheaper? Sort of a bundle price as we have already bought the phone?" Mary said.

"Maybe. I don't have here. It's back at my flat. Will I go and get?"

"Well, I'd like to see it. Why don't we come with you to your place and save you a journey? Then if it's all OK, we can go and get the cash for you," Mary said.

"OK. Let's go."

On the way to Matis' flat, the two detectives tried their best to get as much information as possible from Matis without much success. They did learn that he was originally from Lithuania, and had come to Ireland for work, although he didn't tell them what particular enterprise it was in which he was currently engaged.

Mary Costelloe walked beside Matis as they made their way through the narrow lanes off Shop Street and Liam walked behind, as there was only room on the footpaths for two people side by side. Several times as they encountered street furniture and other pedestrians, Mary brushed up against Matis in a slightly provocative manner.

They turned into Buttermilk Walk, and Matis stopped at a rather weather-beaten red door, sandwiched between a chemist's and an organic food outlet. He opened the door to reveal a wooden staircase that had at one time been carpeted, the sides of the steps still showing traces of cream coloured paint. But the stairs were now bare wood, and the spindles running up the side of it were badly chipped. A single low wattage light bulb was doing its best to illuminate the dreary hallway where several items of junk mail were scattered on the floor.

Matis climbed the stairs quickly, and at the first landing, let himself in to a room on the left-hand side, which Costelloe and Walsh calculated must have been over the organic food shop.

They followed Matis into the room, which was gloomy as the tattered curtains were still pulled across the window. The room smelled stale and unaired, and although it was relatively tidy, everything in it had seen better days. The bed was made, and at the other side of the room, some very basic cooking and washing arrangements stood against the wall. There were no dirty dishes in the sink, but three plates and two cups were stacked on the draining board where they had been left to dry.

Matis pulled back the curtains to admit a modicum of light through the dirty windows. The only seating available in the room was a moth-eaten easy chair that was upholstered in ghastly green damask, so the two detectives remained standing while Matis got down on all fours and retrieved the laptop from a box under the bed. He handed it to Liam.

Walsh opened the laptop, which looked a good deal fresher than anything else in the room, and pressed the power button. The machine came alive, and presented a familiar Windows welcome screen. He noticed that the computer's battery was registering less than 20% and asked, "Do you have the charger?"

"No. But you get easily in Chinese shop for ten euro. Sorry."

Walsh played with the laptop for a few minutes, bringing up the system specification display, but not venturing into the file system for fear of arousing suspicion.

"Do you think it's any good, Hun?" Costelloe asked looking over his shoulder as he tapped the keys and moved the cursor around the screen using the touchpad.

"Yeah, it's not bad. Would do nicely for your student work, but it's a pity about the charger. Have you got the paperwork, Matis?"

"Paperwork – what paperwork?"

"Oh, you know, the guarantee, the receipt, that sort of thing in case anything goes wrong with it?"

"No, sorry. It was my brother's, and he has gone now, back home. But it's good value and nearly new. You won't have need for guarantee."

"What do you think, Mary?" Walsh said.

Mary looked at Matis, again tilting her head and looking as plaintive as she could manage, "I like it, but what is your very best price for a poor student, Matis?"

"I give you for €250. Last offer. OK?"

"Thanks, Matis. We'll take it. But I need to get the cash from home. Can we come by tomorrow morning and collect it and give you the cash then?" Mary said.

"Not today?"

"No, I'm sorry, I'll have to get my father to transfer the money to my account and then withdraw it tomorrow at an ATM. But I can give you €20 deposit to hold it, and I'll come back tomorrow at eleven o'clock with the balance."

"OK, OK, tomorrow eleven o'clock. Doorbell doesn't work, so call me from outside."

Mary Costelloe took one of her own €20 notes from her jeans pocket and handed it over.

Walsh had turned the laptop over and was making a note of the model number and serial number on a scrap of paper.

"What you doing?" Matis said, his voice a little louder, and a frightened look on his face.

"I need to take a note of the model and serial number so I can get a power pack from the shop for it. The battery is almost out."

The Lithuanian seemed happy with the explanation, much to Walsh's relief.

Without further ado, the two detectives let themselves out onto the street and started walking back in the direction of the Garda Station at Mill Street. Costelloe took the phone out of her pocket carefully, and placed it in a plastic evidence bag.

"Let's not go straight back," Costelloe said, linking arms with her colleague. "Just in case he's following us. Let's go back to the shopping centre and make sure we're on our own."

"Good idea. I thought we were busted when he saw me taking down the serial number," Walsh said.

"Excellent improvisation, Detective. I couldn't have done better myself," said Mary, squeezing his arm affectionately.

Chapter Twelve

Lyons and Hays found each other easily at The Brasserie, without the aid of a rolled-up newspaper. The place was filling up, and there was a nice buzz in the air along with delicious aromas of freshly prepared food.

They sat at the table that they often occupied at lunchtime, near the back of the restaurant where it was just a little quieter than the rest of the place. When they had ordered, Hays said to Lyons, "Well then, to what do I owe the pleasure of your company on this fine bright spring day, Ms Lyons?"

Lyons gave her partner an update on where they were with the case, which in fairness didn't amount to much. She also told him that she was feeling quite frustrated with the whole thing, and was hoping that he might be able to give her a few ideas on how best to proceed.

"What's the Dutchman like?" Hays said.

"He's OK. Seems nice enough, but I'm not under any illusion as to why he's here," Lyons said.

"And that would be?"

"He wants to crack this organised crime gang that are up to no good with all this gold. But frankly, I couldn't give a damn about what the Lithuanians are up to in the Netherlands. All I want is to solve this murder case."

"I see what you mean, but maybe as the two could be connected, you could help each other to sort both things out?"

"Maybe. But let's focus on the murder for a minute. I don't think the answer lies in Utrecht. Sure, there may be a connection, but the killing happened here. So who's behind it? We can see the motive clearly enough – obviously the gold. The means is not in dispute, it's just the 'who' that we need to get to."

Hays could sense Lyons' frustration in the way she was telling the story, but just then their food arrived, and Hays hoped that she would feel a bit more positive when she had eaten. After a few mouthfuls, he ventured, "Well, there is one way you might be able to flush them out – but it's risky."

"Go on."

"You could set up a sting. Get someone to buy some of the gold off the net and wait for the thieves to come around to collect. You might not nab the murderer, but it could get you a lot further than you are now."

"Hmm, sounds reasonable. But it could take a while, and consume lots and lots of your valuable budget," Lyons said.

"Let me worry about that. Why don't you have a chat with Janssen about it – he might have something useful to add, and he could give you an idea of the lead time between the gold being sent and it being taken back – if that's actually what is happening."

"Have you some doubt about it?"

"Yeah, I do. It's a nice story, but it sounds a bit – I don't know – wacky. It's too easy. I'd say there's a bit more to it if you ask me. There's another dimension to the whole thing that Janssen either doesn't know about, or isn't telling you. Why don't you have dinner with him? Get him to lower his guard a bit, see if you can get him to open up about what's really going on?" Hays said.

"You wouldn't mind?"

"You don't have to sleep with him! Just soften him up. Use the old Maureen Lyons charm on the man. He'll be putty in your hands!"

"OK. I'll see what I can do."

* * *

When Lyons got back to the station, Janssen was there sitting in the open plan. She asked him into her office.

"How did you get on at the morgue?" she said.

"Yes, well it is as I thought. The method of her killing is textbook Lithuanian gangs. The stabbing is optional though."

"Lovely. Why do you think she was killed anyway?" Lyons said.

"I would say that the killer had some kind of falling out with her, quite possibly over the amount she was prepared to pay for the gold he had collected. These fellows are very greedy. I suspect they had an argument, and it got out of hand, and she was killed."

"So, now there is a Lithuanian gangster on the loose who has a stash of gold in his possession, and probably a contract on his head. We can expect more violence before this is over, yes?"

"Possibly, but that depends on how good you are at catching whoever did it. Catch him, or them, and it will put an end to it, at least as far as Galway is concerned," Janssen said.

"How long are you planning to stay in Galway, Inspector Janssen?"

"I'm not sure. A couple more days, I guess."

"Well, would you like us to go to dinner later on? You could sample some of our famous *haute cuisine* at the expense of the Irish taxpayer."

"Thank you, that would be very nice. You are very kind," he said, smiling warmly.

"No problem. Why don't I pick you up at the Imperial Hotel at seven thirty? I'll book somewhere nice." Lyons stood up, indicating to Janssen that their meeting was over, and that she expected him to leave and go back to his hotel. Not wanting to prevail too much on the Gardaí's hospitality, he took the hint, and departed.

Lyons was glad to have a few minutes to herself to think over the idea that Hays had suggested at lunch. Who could she get to buy gold on-line, that would be willing to be robbed soon afterwards? Not an easy one. They would have to be completely independent of anything to do with the Gardaí, because the sellers would undoubtedly check into their customer quite extensively in an effort to avoid a sting. She did have a person in mind, but some more thought was needed.

* * *

When she went back to the main office, Walsh and Costelloe had just arrived back in. They had dropped the iPhone and the serial number of the laptop off at forensics to see if Sinéad Loughran's team could get any prints or

105

trace evidence from them, and were excited about the prospect. If it turned out to be Geller's property, then it could well be that Matis was involved, or maybe even he himself was the killer.

They told Lyons and Flynn about the plan to return to Buttermilk Lane the following morning to get the laptop.

"Do you think he was suspicious of you at all? We don't want to expose you two to any risks," Flynn said.

"I don't think so. He was very keen on the money, although he did go a bit funny when Liam started taking down the serial number of the laptop. But Liam was quick on his feet, and made a credible excuse."

"Hmm. Well, let's see what Sinéad comes back with. If she gets a trace, or a print from Geller, we'll turn up mob handed in the morning and bring him in. Good work guys, well done. Now, anyone got anything else – Sally, Eamon?" Lyons said.

Everyone looked down at the floor, and no one said a word.

"Terrific! C'mon folks – for heaven's sake – let's get a bit of energy into this. A woman has been murdered, and there may be more to follow if we don't get a shift on. Has anyone checked the list of houses broken into over the last year in the area, especially out west? We need to correlate the victim profiles, see if we can detect a pattern. Get onto all the stations in the area and speak to the Officer in Charge. John, you can build a database or whatever you call it, and do some analysis. I want the information on my desk first thing, so you'd better get to it," she said. She stomped off back to her own office. It wasn't fair to take the lack of progress out on her team, who she knew to be dedicated and diligent, but this case was really getting her down, and if someone else came to grief because they hadn't made sufficient progress, she would feel very bad indeed.

Lyons spent what was left of the afternoon on her PC researching Lithuanian organised crime and anything she could find about gold theft or smuggling involving eastern Europe and beyond. There was plenty to discover. Time and time again, as she delved into the details, connections with the far east, and China in particular, kept popping up. She discovered that China had become the world's largest producer of gold, overtaking South Africa in around 2007. Output was now almost 500 tonnes annually – more than twice as much as its nearest rival, and it was still rising steadily. It was hardly surprising that the criminal classes had become involved. After over an hour ploughing around a host of different web sites, she managed to put together a simplistic trail, following the gold from its production to the scam that was taking place on her own home ground.

A great deal of Chinese gold is distributed out through Hong Kong. And so, co-incidentally, are vast quantities of cheap manufactured goods made on the mainland of China. Smuggling small, but significant quantities, of the metal that had been skimmed off from the mines or smelting processes was a simple task. It could be easily disguised in among all the other shipments travelling west in containers.

Once the gold was out of China, an elaborate chain of handlers passed it on from one place to another till it arrived at a foundry where it was fashioned into ingots varying in weight from 25 grams up to one kilo, or in some cases, even 10 kilo bars. It was the smaller ones that were sold as retail on the web, embossed with fraudulent markings.

Lyons didn't notice the time slipping past, and before she knew it, it was after seven o'clock.

"Cripes," she said to herself, "no time to go home and put on the glad rags. I'll just have to go as I am."

She did make time to go to the bathroom and freshen up, and apply a small layer of subtle makeup and a dart of expensive perfume, before she left the station.

Lyons parked her new Volvo in the set down area in front of the Imperial Hotel, and put the laminated Garda sign that she had had made in the windscreen to fend off any zealous parking attendants that might still be cruising the busy streets around Eyre Square at that hour.

She met up with Luuk Janssen in the lobby of the hotel as arranged. He was looking dapper, having put on a crisp white shirt and silk tie which he wore under a navy blazer with brass buttons.

"Hi. Ready for off?" Lyons said cheerily as Janssen arose to greet her.

"Yes, thank you. This is very kind of you. I'm sure you would prefer to be at home after a long day."

She would of course have preferred just that, but she responded differently.

"No, not at all. It's not often we get to exchange information with our European colleagues, and get to know a bit about how policing is done in other jurisdictions. Anyway, I'm hungry, so let's go."

Lyons had booked the two of them into the restaurant on the top floor of the Great Southern Hotel, on the other side of the square from the Imperial. As they crossed Eyre Square, Lyons told Janssen that it had now been renamed

John F Kennedy park, in honour of the unfortunate American president whom the Irish had claimed for their own. She also showed him the statue of Pádraic Ó Conaire, the celebrated Irish writer who was widely acclaimed for his works on Irish contemporary life at the end of the 19th and start of the 20th centuries.

When they reached the restaurant, the head waiter, Michael Bennett, greeted Lyons by name and showed the two of them to a larger than normal two-seater table with a magnificent view out over the city. The table was set with a crisp white linen tablecloth and matching serviettes, and the highly polished silver-plated cutlery and cut crystal glassware sparkled in the light from the candle that was already lit and flickering in the centre.

"This is magnificent," Janssen said as he took his seat.

"Yes, it's one of the best views in Galway, and the food is pretty good too. They also have a terrific wine list. May I ask you to choose?" Lyons said.

"It would be my pleasure, Inspector. Do you prefer red or white?"

"I'll leave that up to you, Luuk – is it OK to call you Luuk by the way?"

"Yes, of course. I'm sorry, I didn't catch your first name," Janssen said, a little embarrassed by his own lack of observation.

"Maureen, that's me."

As the meal progressed, the two detectives talked of their respective jobs, and some of the cases they had worked on.

"What particular aspect of crime in the Netherlands are you involved in, Luuk?" Lyons asked as their empty soup plates were being taken away.

"These days, I specialize in organized crime mostly, though Utrecht is not a big place, so we all lend a hand with whatever is going on at the time. But I've just finished with a currency forgery case. It involved dollars that were being printed in North Korea – Superdollars, they call them, because they are said to be better than the real thing. Utrecht was being used as a distribution centre for them, and we managed to round up a pretty nasty gang and put them away."

"Nice. Did you recover much of the forged currency?"

"We got just over two million, but that's only a small portion of the amount that is actually produced. It is calculated that there is as much as $500 million of counterfeit US dollars in circulation at any time, so a drop in the sea really."

"Sounds like a significant haul, all the same. What sentence will the forgers get?"

"Probably ten years or more. There were some other quite violent crimes involved as well that I'd rather not tell you about over a nice meal," Janssen said.

Just as their beef wellington arrived and was placed in front of them, Lyons' work phone began to ring in her bag.

"Damn. Excuse me, I'll have to answer this," she said. She reached down to her bag which was on the floor, and turning slightly away from the Dutch policeman, answered the call.

"Lyons."

"Hello, boss. It's Eamon here. Can I ask where you are?"

"I'm in the Great Southern, why?"

"Oh, sorry. Look, there's been what we think is a shooting here in Buttermilk Walk. Details are a bit sketchy for now. I'm on my way down there. I thought you should know," Flynn said.

"How certain are you it's actually a shooting?"

"Well, a neighbour called it in. She lives in a bedsit over a shop and she heard a row followed by what she said was a single shot coming from the bedsit on the other side of the landing about fifteen minutes ago. Then she heard someone running down the stairs and out onto the street."

"Did she get a look at whoever it was?"

"No, she was too scared to look. But we'll know more when we get there."

"OK. I'm on my way. Which end of the street is it?"

"It's between the chemists and the food shop – a red door. You'll see us outside in any case with the blue lights."

"OK. See you in about ten minutes, oh, and I'll have Inspector Janssen with me," Lyons said.

"Fine," Flynn replied, wondering what she was doing with the visitor at eight o'clock at night.

Chapter Thirteen

Lyons used the blue lights to get past the squad car that was stopped across the entrance to Buttermilk Walk. She drove slowly down the narrow street where a number of onlookers had gathered to see what all the fuss was about.

There was a uniformed Garda that she recognised guarding the door of the premises where the incident had occurred, and she gave her name, and that of Inspector Janssen to him, which he duly recorded.

The room that had been occupied by Matis Vitkus was crowded with people. Flynn was there along with Mary Costelloe, and a paramedic was still hovering around what was clearly the dead body of the Lithuanian. Vitkus had been shot once in the head – a clean shot at close range. There was a spray of blood and brain matter on the wall behind where the assassination had taken place, and a nasty looking knife lay beside the man's body on the floor.

"Shit! What a mess," Lyons said to no one in particular. "Eamon, can you get the uniforms started on house-to-house along the street, somebody may have seen the killer making his escape."

"Already underway, boss. I haven't interviewed the girl from opposite yet – Mary is with her. She's pretty shook up. Do you want to talk to her?" Flynn asked.

"Yes, I'll do that in a minute. Has someone called Dr Dodd?"

"Yes. I did. He's on his way, and so is Sinéad Loughran," Flynn said.

"Thanks. Oh, and can you have a look around and see if you can find a laptop computer? If you do, bag it up carefully. Mary and Liam were supposed to be buying it from him tomorrow morning. We think it might have belonged to Geller," Lyons said.

"Sure. No problem. What about….?" Flynn said, nodding his head towards the door where Inspector Janssen was standing.

"I'll deal with that." But before she could, Janssen spoke up, "I think I should leave you to get on with this, Inspector. I'll go back to my hotel. May I call around in the morning?"

"Yes, thanks Luuk. Of course. I'll be in from eight o'clock at the latest."

As Luuk Janssen was making his way down the narrow stairs to the front door, Dr Julian Dodd was attempting to come up. Janssen saw him coming, and retreated to allow the doctor to make his entrance.

"Greetings, Maureen, and what have you got me out for this time?" Dodd said in his usual slightly superior tone.

"Good evening, Doctor," she said, pointing to the lifeless form of Matis Vitkus on the floor beside the bed.

"Well at least this one isn't in the back of beyond!" Dodd got down on his knees and made a cursory examination of the body. He felt in vain for a pulse, and moved the man's head from side to side, being careful not to get blood on his clothing. After a moment or two, Dodd struggled to his feet again.

"Well, what do you think, doctor?" Lyons said.

"Whoever he is, he's definitely dead, but you knew that anyway. Why they need me to certify life extinct is beyond me, but there you go."

"And any idea of time of death, doctor?"

Eamon Flynn flicked through his pocket book and said, "The shot was reported at 8:34, boss."

"I'd say approximately 8:34, inspector, or a few minutes before that, wouldn't you say?" Dodd said. Lyons was used to his acerbic comments, so she ignored the jibe.

"What about the gun? Any sign of the bullet?"

"You'll have to get forensics to have a dig around for it. It's almost certainly not lodged in the head judging by the splatter on the wall. I'll be doing the post-mortem tomorrow morning, and we'll know more then. If that's all, I'll leave you to it."

The good doctor departed, and Lyons went across the hall to talk to the girl who had called in the gunshot, leaving the paramedics to scoop up the remains of Matis Vitkus, and Flynn and Loughran to start a thorough search of the room.

* * *

Paulina Mazur was a slight, blonde girl with shoulder length hair and a long narrow face. She was Polish, and worked in one of the hotels on the edge of town as a cleaner, despite the fact that she had actually qualified as a

114

school teacher in Lublin, near her home town. The events of the evening had taken their toll on the girl. Her complexion was now ashen, and she was trembling visibly.

Mary Costelloe was doing what she could to comfort her, and had managed to find some tea bags and a couple of clean mugs in what was a rather untidy space occupied by the Pole. The room was a mirror image of the one that Matis had stayed in, but much less orderly, with clothing strewn around untidily, dirty dishes in the sink, and several pairs of shoes scattered around the floor. The bed was unmade.

When Lyons came in, Mary Costelloe made the introductions and then excused herself.

Lyons sat down at the small table, and spoke softly to the girl.

"I know this is difficult for you, Paulina, but could I just ask you to go over what happened here earlier?"

"Is he dead, the man?" Paulina said.

"Yes, yes I'm afraid so. It was quick – he didn't suffer. Did you know him well?"

"No, hardly at all. He was a very private person. We just said hello if we met on the stairs, that's all."

"So, what happened this evening then?"

"I got home from work at about 6:45. I was tired after a twelve hour shift, so I lay down on the bed for a short nap before getting food. Some time after, I was woken by shouting coming from over there," the girl said nervously.

"Were both men shouting?"

"Yes, both. But I couldn't make out what they were saying. Then it all went quiet for a few minutes, and then, then…"

"It's OK, Paulina, take your time. Then you heard a shot. Is that right?" Lyons said.

"Yes, I guess," she said, wringing her hands together. Her eyes were full of tears, and Lyons handed her a tissue from her handbag.

"What did you do when you heard the gun go off?"

"I wasn't sure what it was. I have never heard a gun being fired like that. But after a minute, I guessed that something bad had happened, and I called your 999. I was too scared to go out onto the landing."

"Did the man leave Matis' room immediately?"

"Not immediately. Maybe three or four minutes later. I heard him running down the stairs very fast and out the door."

"Did you see this man at all – the one running away?"

"No. I was afraid to look. Even after he was gone and it was all quiet, I stayed in here until the police came to the door. I was very frightened."

"Have you ever seen Matis with any other men at all, Paulina?"

"No, never. I only see him rarely, and he is always alone. What will happen to me now? Will I be sent home?" Paulina asked.

"Of course not. You have done nothing wrong. I will ask you to come into the police station tomorrow to make a statement. But if you remember anything – anything at all, no matter how small – please let me know, and thank you for your help," Lyons said, handing the girl a business card and getting up to leave.

"Irish police are nicer than ours in Poland," Paulina said, managing a smile.

Back in Matis' room, the forensic team were finishing their meticulous search of the small area. They had taken fingerprints from all around, and were removing the cups that had been left out in case some saliva DNA might be recovered from them. Sinéad Loughran stood up as Lyons came back in.

"Hi, Maureen. We found the bullet. It was lodged in the bed leg. It's badly mashed, but we may be able to get some information from it," she said.

"Well, that's something, I suppose. Any sign of his passport or papers?"

"No, not a trace. I reckon the killer must have taken them with him to slow down the identification process. He can't have been aware that Matis was known to us already."

"What about the laptop? We know he had it here, because he was going to sell it to Mary and Liam tomorrow at eleven," Lyons said.

"No, nothing there either, and we've had a good look."

"OK. I want you to go through the kitchen waste – look for anything at all that might be helpful to us in connecting Matis up to whoever else he was involved with. He must have left some traces behind. Have you been through his pockets?"

"Yes. €250 in cash and some change, a dirty handkerchief. A Post-it note with some numbers on it, and two wrapped mint sweets – the kind they give you in a restaurant at the end of your meal."

"Right. I'm going down to see if the neighbours saw anyone. Let me know if you find anything of interest, thanks."

Back down on the street, Lyons met Eamon Flynn who was directing operations.

"Hi, Eamon. Anything from the door-to-door?"

"Sorry, boss. Nothing so far. I see the Chemist has a CCTV camera pointed at the door. But it's inside the shop, and it would have been closed at the time of the incident, or so it says in the window in any case."

"Well, dig out the keyholder anyway. Mill Street should have a record of whoever it is. I want that CCTV analysed tonight if it was still recording. And let's have a briefing at 08:00 tomorrow with everyone."

"Right, boss," Flynn said, knowing that Lyons was in no mood to be challenged.

Lyons drove back to the Imperial and parked again in the set down area in front of the hotel. She found Janssen sitting at the bar on his own with two thirds of a pint of Guinness in front of him. She sat up on one of the high chairs beside him.

"Ah, Maureen. What can I get you?" Janssen asked.

"Oh, just a soda water please, I'm still on duty."

"How are things down at the house?"

"We're not much further on, I'm afraid." She explained how little they had discovered. She also told Janssen about the plan to buy the computer, and the fact that it had now gone missing.

"Well, robbery wasn't the prime motive for the killing. Otherwise the cash would have been taken. But this has all the signs of a clean-up operation by the gang," he said.

"How do you mean?"

"Vitkus was obviously getting into a little business of his own, selling off the phone and the laptop like that.

That would be what they refer to as a loose end, and would need to be taken care of. And it was."

"But does that mean that Vitkus murdered Maria Geller?"

"No, but it's a possibility. More likely he was selling the stolen stuff for someone else – a friend. Are you certain the phone belonged to Maria Geller?"

"No, we're not. But I'll know first thing tomorrow morning. Forensics have it and are going over it carefully for trace evidence. Would you like to come in at eight o'clock tomorrow and sit in on our meeting?" Lyons said.

"Yes, I would very much. And I'll see if I can find out anything in the meantime about your latest victim."

"What? At this time of night?"

"Yes, of course. Our computers never sleep!"

Lyons said goodnight to Luuk Janssen and left the hotel. When she got back out to the car, she sent a text to Sinéad Loughran asking her to attend the briefing the following morning. There was nothing more she could do that night, so reluctantly, she went home.

Chapter Fourteen

Lyons had persuaded her partner to sit in on the briefing the following morning. With two murders unsolved, and no real clues except for some vague information about gold theft and smuggling, she felt the need for his insight into the case. She was hoping that his greater experience would be able to provide some new direction for the investigation.

Hays had agreed to join the team for the briefing, but made it clear that he was expecting Lyons to lead. He would stay out of it, unless something occurred to him that they hadn't thought of.

Lyons got the meeting underway just after eight. Janssen had turned up, as promised, a few minutes earlier, and was nursing a small paper cup full of what looked like hot treacle.

"I think you all know Inspector Janssen from the Dutch police by now. Out of courtesy, I'll ask Inspector Janssen to tell us what he has found out so far," she said.

"Thank you for your consideration, Inspector Lyons. In fact, I have discovered quite a lot overnight. I used various IT systems that we can access to burrow a little deeper into our friend Matis."

"Oh, and what did you discover?" Lyons asked.

"Well, firstly, his name is not Vitkus. He was born Mateus Vidas in Akmenyne, on the border between Lithuania and Belarus. Of course, this was all part of the USSR at that time. He's wanted in several countries by the police, largely for petty crimes, but more latterly for more serious matters involving money laundering. I think he must have come to Ireland to avoid unpleasantness back home, but it looks like it caught up with him in any case."

"Thank you, Inspector, that's very useful. Is there anything else?" Lyons said.

"Well, I have a list of his known associates. It's not very long – he was a bit of a loner," Janssen said, holding up a piece of paper.

"Great. John, can you take this and get onto our colleagues in Dublin? See if any of them have come into the country recently." Lyons handed the list to John O'Connor who went over to a quiet corner of the room to make the call.

"Sinéad – have you got anything for us?" Lyons said.

"Well, the iPhone did, it seems, belong to Maria Geller. We found skin particles in the charging port, and small traces of blood wedged down the side of the screen. The specimens are very small, so some further verification is needed, but I'd put this month's salary on it being hers. Then, about the other death in Buttermilk Way, the killer was quite careless. He left boot prints and saliva traces on the coffee mug, but no actual fingerprints that we can attribute specifically to him. We did find the bullet shell though – it had rolled under the bed, so we're still working on that to get more information. We have the actual bullet as well, though it is pretty bashed up. The killer will have powder scorches on his hands and on his clothing though, so if we can find him quickly, we might be able to tie him in."

"Thanks, Sinéad. When you've finished with the phone, can you give it to John so he can see if he can get anything from it? And what about the knife? Anything there?" Lyons said.

"Just Vitkus' fingerprints, boss, and it doesn't look as if it has been used."

"Ok, thanks Sinéad. Anything from the CCTV in the chemists, Eamon?"

"We got the keyholder out, and they gave us the CD from the system. It's handy – it records when there's any movement, so it can run for days if things are quiet before it overwrites. We've had a brief look, and we can see someone emerging from the door of the flat at about the time the incident was called in, but they have a hoodie on, and they're all dressed in black, so no identification, I'm afraid," Flynn said.

"Damn. Can you see if there's any other cameras working on Buttermilk Walk? The chemist's is surely not the only one. What about the scrap of paper found in the victim's pocket – anything there?" Lyons said.

"We're still trying to figure out what the numbers are, boss," Sinéad Loughran said.

At this point Janssen put up his hand.

"Yes, Luuk, go ahead."

"I was just thinking; these people often have several passports. If you could get your friends at the airport to provide a list of everyone who has arrived recently with a Lithuanian passport, I could run the names and see if any aliases pop up."

"Excellent!" Lyons said. She looked over to where John O'Connor was standing and he nodded.

"I'm on it, boss."

Then Lyons took a sheet of paper out of her folder.

"This is a list – a rather short list – of reported burglaries in this area where gold items were reported stolen. It mostly concerns jewellery. I'm not convinced that this is the extent of the robberies. Sally, can you get onto the home insurance companies? There are only three or four that cover the region. Ask for the claims manager, and see if we can get details of any claims involving jewellery, gold or whatever, and cross reference it to this list. We'll have a look at that later. What about the numbers on the Post-it note Matis had in his trouser pocket? Eamon – can you follow up on that, see if you can make any sense of it? Let's reconvene after lunch and see how we're getting on. Oh, Liam, Mary, can you go across to the post-mortem on Matis and see what emerges, if anything? And don't let Dr Dodd's rather sarcastic manner intimidate you. He's a fine pathologist, just a bit quirky," Lyons said.

Hays, who had remained silent throughout the meeting, now spoke up as the group started to disperse.

"Inspector Janssen, I wonder if we could have a word in Maureen's office?" he said.

"Yes, of course, sir."

Lyons, Hays and Janssen withdrew to Lyons' office. When they were all seated around Lyons' desk, Hays spoke to Janssen.

"Inspector Janssen, I'm not sure if Inspector Lyons has explained my role in these cases to you. I'm the superintendent in charge of the detective units for the region, and to put it bluntly, I'm getting quite a lot of heat from on high with two unsolved murders on my patch. And now, it seems, there is some connection with international organised crime. This is not what we are used to in these parts. If there is anything you can do – anything at all – to help us solve these dreadful crimes quickly, it would be greatly appreciated. The last thing we need is this sort of thing taking hold around here."

"Yes, of course, Superintendent. I'll do anything I can to help, and you can help me too," Janssen said.

"Oh, how come? In what way can we help?" Hays said.

"I didn't mention this earlier, because I didn't think it would be helpful, but the way these people work may involve more of the locals than you think. In order to help avoid detection, the criminals that sell the gold often set up some kind of local distribution. If they can send out the gold by post from within the target country, then there is no issue with customs or anything like that. All they have to worry about is getting the gold into the local area in bulk, which is usually done by including it within some other innocuous cargo. We discovered such an arrangement in the Netherlands, which is how I became involved. The gold was being hidden in consignments of ordinary everyday household items from China. It's so small and easy to hide that it wasn't discovered by routine inspections. We found 100 small ingots inside a shipment of kitchen utensils. That's nearly half a million euros worth."

"I see. So, you think that there is someone in Ireland receiving quantities of gold and then posting it out to people who buy it on the net?" Lyons said.

"Quite possibly. And that's the beauty of it. He or she probably doesn't know anything about the gold being stolen and sent back to the main distributors in eastern Europe. Very few of the players know each other, which protects the gang from leakage," Janssen said.

"But then why kill Geller and this Matis character?" Hays said.

"Collateral damage. Maybe she got careless, or decided to help herself to a slice. Or maybe they just killed her to keep the others on their toes. These gangs are brutal – they have no regard for human life."

"And Matis – why do you think he was killed?" Lyons asked.

"I need to do some more work on that before I can explain it. I don't think he killed Geller though. I'm not sure, but I think he may have been just an opportunist who bought the phone and the laptop in a pub for a few euros and was selling them on for profit. But we'll see. If I can spend some more time using your computers, I may be able to make some headway with it," Janssen said.

"Yes, of course. Help yourself. John O'Connor will log you in. He's our technologist," Hays said.

"Thank you. That's most helpful. Is there anything else?" Janssen said.

"No, that's all for now, Inspector. Thanks for your help," Hays said.

Janssen got up and left the office to go in search of John O'Connor.

"What do you think, Mick?" Lyons said.

"I don't know. It's more complex than the cases we're used to. And if it's true what he says, then there's a lot more work to do before we get to the bottom of it. Are you OK with it all?"

"Sort of. I have a few ideas that might be worth following up. We'll see."

"Care to share?" Hays said.

"No, not yet. Let's see if anything comes of them first. It could be a wild goose chase and I don't want to embarrass myself in front of a senior officer!"

"Hmph. Right, OK if I leave you to it then? I've got a flaming juvenile crime meeting with social services in half an hour, and I'd better at least appear that I know what I'm talking about."

"Riveting stuff!" Lyons said. She came out from behind the desk and gave him a quick kiss on the lips.

"See you later then."

* * *

When Hays had left the room, Lyons picked up the phone and called Séan Mulholland in Clifden.

"Hi, Séan. Look, I think I may have found a way for Peadar Tobin to redeem himself. Is he on duty this morning?"

"Yes, he is. He's just gone down town. A tourist has had their motorbike stolen from outside the Station House Hotel. Why?"

"I have a little job for him. I don't want to talk about it on the phone. Can you get him to meet me in the hotel in Oughterard in forty-five minutes?" Lyons said.

"I suppose so. What's it about?" Mulholland said.

"I'll tell you after, Séan, if it works out. Sorry, but it's a bit of a long shot."

"Oh, right so. I'll call him on the radio and get him into Oughterard for ye."

"Thanks, Séan. See ya."

Lyons found Eamon Flynn and told him that she had to go out, and if she wasn't back by two o'clock, he was to take the afternoon meeting.

Flynn agreed, and asked her where she was going, but she wouldn't say.

Lyons enjoyed the drive out to Oughterard in her new Volvo. Mid-morning was the best time to travel from a traffic perspective, and once she was clear of the city, she let the car out, enjoying the lively acceleration and good handling that it provided.

She found Tobin in the lounge of the hotel relaxing with a cup of coffee. Somehow, he had managed to change out of his uniform, and was wearing a pair of navy slacks, a tweed sports jacket, but still had his blue Garda shirt on.

Tobin stood up as Lyons entered the lounge.

"Hello, Inspector. Can I get you a coffee or something?" he said.

"Thanks, Peadar. Yes, a cappuccino would be great."

Tobin caught the eye of the waitress and ordered Lyons' coffee.

"Thanks for coming in, Peadar. I guess you have some idea what this is about."

"Well, I suppose it's something to do with the murder out at Owen Glen. I'm sorry about that business with McCutcheon. I didn't know it would lead to trouble."

"I think Séan is looking after that for us. But there have been some fairly significant developments since."

Lyons brought Tobin up to date, telling him most of what Janssen had revealed, and of course outlining the events surrounding the second murder.

"God, that's a right old mess, all right. So, how can I help, Inspector?"

"I'd like you to take yourself out to Westport and befriend one of the girls working at the Eurosaver shop. I'd like to know if there's anything going on there – it doesn't feel quite right to me," Lyons said.

"What's bothering you about it?"

"McCutcheon seems to have more money and assets than a pound shop could reasonably deliver. I know he gets his stock dirt cheap, but still – there's a limited market for that stuff and Westport only has so many customers. So, I think there may be something else going on."

"OK. Is there any evidence to suggest what it might be?"

"No, no there isn't. Call it intuition or whatever you like, that's why we'll have to be very discreet. I don't want McCutcheon to know we are investigating him. You'll need a bit of time off if this is going to work. I'll square that with Séan for you. Are you in?" Lyons asked.

"I am to be sure. It'll be a bit of a diversion from shop-lifting and speeding tickets," he said, smiling.

"Good man. Don't be too obvious with your questioning if you do manage to hit it off with one of the girls. Play it cool."

"You can count on me, Inspector. Don't worry. If there's anything going on, I'll find out what it is. And thanks for the opportunity."

"Think of it as making amends for doing nixers, Peadar. I'm sure you've told McCutcheon that all that's finished with?"

"Oh, I have, of course. There wasn't much in it anyway, to be honest, just a few quid now and then when something went wrong up at the Glen. I put him on to another friend of mine, not in the Guards. I told him with summer coming on I'd be too busy to keep it up, and he didn't question it."

"Good. Right, well that's it. Let me know how you get on. I'll text you my mobile number – oh, and not a word to anyone about this, and you report back to me and me only. Understood?"

"Yes, no problem."

Lyons got up to leave, and Tobin stood up too.

"Thanks for the coffee. Talk soon," Lyons said.

As she drove back to the city, she hoped that this little side-show wouldn't backfire on her.

* * *

When Lyons returned to the station, Eamon Flynn knocked on her door.

"Come in, Eamon. What's up?"

"I think we may have had a bit of luck, boss. I was down on Buttermilk Walk earlier, looking for more CCTV cameras, as you suggested. As I was looking around, a man came out of one of the buildings and we got chatting. He was asking me what all the fuss was about, so I gave him some brief details. He had a nice new black Mercedes parked at the side of the road, and when I asked him about CCTV on the street, he told me that his car had a dash-cam that recorded all the time if there was any movement near the car. He had installed it after his previous Mercedes had been vandalised in the very same spot."

"Interesting. Was it any use?"

"Yes, it was. He gave us the little memory card out of it and I brought it back to John. It had recorded what looks like our man coming towards the car, and getting into an old Nissan Micra parked a few places in front of the Merc," Flynn said.

"Nice one. Any useable facial shots? Did we get the number of the Micra?" Lyons said, now excited by this development.

"We got quite a good facial picture. John did a bit of work on it to enhance the definition, and he's given a print of it to Inspector Janssen. The camera didn't capture the reg number of the Micra though. Oh, and there's more."

"Go on."

"Sinéad did some more work on the bullet and shell casing we found at the scene. It appears that the gun used is an old Russian military service revolver – probably a Makarov IZH-70 or 71. It may have a built-in suppressor to make it a bit quieter. Just the job if you want to bump off someone in an occupied building."

"Excellent. So, now we have identified the weapon; we have a mug shot of Matis' killer; we have his DNA; how hard can it be to find the bugger? I want you to get Liam, Mary and Sally out and about with the photo of this guy's face. Get them to go around all the places where the eastern Europeans congregate and make it clear that this is a serious business. We might be able to get someone to talk. Get them to lay it on thick – you know the drill – deportation, incarceration – put the frighteners on and let's see what shakes loose. Tell them to hint at a reward for information too, but not to be specific," Lyons said.

"Right, boss, nothing like a bit of carrot and stick! I'll see to it."

Lyons made her way back out to the open plan where Garda John O'Connor and Inspector Luuk Janssen were huddled over a PC screen. She walked up behind them for a look, but was surprised to find that the text on the PC was in a language she didn't recognise.

"What's up, John?" she said.

"Inspector Janssen is consulting an overseas database that he has access to, to see if he can identify our mystery man from Buttermilk Walk."

"Cool. Any luck Inspector?"

"Give me another half hour or so and I think I will have some information," he said not lifting his eyes from the screen.

"OK. We'll have a meeting then with the whole team."

Chapter Fifteen

The meeting started at five o'clock. The team that had been sent out around the city were back. Lyons asked for an update from Sally Fahy to kick things off.

"Nothing, boss. I'm sure one or two of them recognised the man in the photo, but no one was saying anything. They're scared," Fahy said.

"How do you know they recognised the guy?" Flynn said.

"Just the way they looked at the pic and then avoided eye contact with me – you get to know the signs."

Janssen was just finishing up at O'Connor's PC, and he came across to take his seat and join the rest of them.

"Inspector, I think I may have something."

"Yes, Inspector, go ahead," Lyons said.

"I took the photo from the man's dash camera, and sent it to colleagues in Utrecht who used it to search some databases. They came up with a hit for a man with several identities, and who is known to be a very serious criminal."

"Do you have a name, Luuk?" Lyons asked.

"Many names I'm afraid. He appears to have a number of passports, but he often travels under the name of Dieter Essig which may actually be his name, we don't know for sure. He has eluded capture for a number of years now, even though there are many warrants out for his arrest, so he is extremely clever."

"Do we have a better photograph from your colleagues, Luuk?" Flynn said.

"We have a number, because he changes his appearance from time to time. Sometimes he has blonde hair, sometimes dark. Sometimes clean shaven, sometimes with a beard. But at present, he is fair and clean shaven according to the car picture."

"Right, thanks Luuk, that's terrific. Eamon, we need to get moving on this new information immediately. Circulate the best photo from the ones we now have, and alert all the ports and airports. Get back to the eastern European community too and put some serious pressure on. Let's see if we can flush him out. Oh, and get uniform to handbill the town too. I'll get Séan to do the same in Clifden, and we can get Westport on the job as well. Sally, can we do anything about his car?"

"We can try, boss, but without a reg number, it's not going to be easy. There are hundreds of those Micras in Galway, but I can put the word out, and see if we can get anything."

The meeting broke up, with members of the team going about their assigned tasks. Lyons withdrew to her office for some thinking time. Janssen looked in, but saw that she was in no mood to be disturbed, so he went back to his hotel. But he wasn't contemplating a quiet night in watching TV. He had other ideas.

Lyons sketched a sort of mind-map out on her jotter. But try as she would, she couldn't make sense of it. She couldn't connect the events up in any sort of coherent fashion, at least not in a way that would allow the investigation to progress. She wasn't happy, and not for the first time, she questioned her own ability to bring this one in. Feeling thoroughly fed up, she packed up her things, logged out of the PC and left for home.

* * *

Luuk Janssen got back to the hotel just before 6 p.m. and went to his room. He ordered some food and two bottles of Heineken from room service, and changed into some scruffy jeans and a well-worn shirt while he was waiting for it to arrive. When he had eaten, he left the tray outside his room and went down to reception. Here he made some enquiries, and noted down a few bits of information the very helpful man at the desk was only too willing to impart. Then he set off into the cool evening air.

When he arrived at the first place the hotel clerk had given him, it was almost empty. One or two men sat at the bar with pints of Guinness in front of them, but they appeared to be locals, as far as Janssen could determine from their conversation. He ordered a sparkling water and sat up at the bar, keen to engage the bartender in conversation.

His further enquiries yielded some more names of pubs in the seedier side of town, and two of them matched ones he had been given at the hotel. He got directions, and left half the water behind, leaving the barman perplexed.

The next establishment was much busier. Again, he ordered fizzy water, and found a seat close to a group of noisy young men who were definitely not local. He eased his way into conversation with the group, and before long it was as if they had been buddies for ever. He bought a round of drinks for them, and after half an hour, ventured that he was interested in buying a cheap laptop computer, if any of them knew how that might be arranged. He made it clear that he wasn't too fussy about the provenance of the item, as long as it was working, and was at the right price. Although the group were a little guarded at this turn in the conversation, another round of drinks soon began to erode their inhibitions, and one of them offered to make a phone call. The young man got up and went outside, returning a few minutes later.

"I think we may have it for you. A man will come. Have you cash ready?" he said to Janssen.

"Yes, no problem. Thank you. If it goes well, I'll give you €20 for your trouble," Jansen said, which seemed to please the youth who beamed at him, and lifted his glass by way of a salute.

Janssen kept the group talking until some minutes later Dieter Essig entered the bar with a small grey laptop computer tucked under his arm.

"Ah, come in Walter, join us, have a drink," one of the young men said to the new arrival. Janssen recognised one of Dieter's aliases.

Essig sat down, and a bottle of beer appeared in front of him. He took a generous swig, and then asked, "Who is buying my PC?" in a pronounced accent.

Janssen told him that he was his customer, and Essig handed the laptop to him. Janssen opened it and turned it on, but the screen only lit up for a moment and then went blank.

"Is it working?" Janssen asked.

"Yes, of course, but I have no charger. It works fine. You can get one on eBay for a few Euros," Essig said.

Janssen closed it again and turned it over, as if to check the condition of the underside. He glimpsed the serial number stamped into the grey plastic, and saw that the last four digits were the same as the ones he had memorised from Walsh's notes earlier at the briefing.

"OK, but I am taking a chance. Two hundred," he said.

Essig reached out to take the laptop back, "No. It is three hundred. If you don't want it, I sell it to someone else." He started to stand up.

"OK, OK," Janssen said quickly, "Jeez man, take it easy."

Jansen reached into his pocket and withdrew six crisp €50 notes and offered them to Essig who appeared to have relaxed a bit when he saw the money. The exchange was made, and Janssen again feigned interest in his new acquisition, without pawing it too much.

Essig got up and said goodbye to the group, eliciting a few moans from them, and calls for him to sit down and have another drink. But a few seconds later he was out the door.

Janssen made his excuses too, and left as soon afterwards as he could.

Once outside, he saw the back of Dieter Essig disappearing down the alley that ran beside the pub they had been in. He followed at a safe distance. At the end of the sparsely lit lane, the road went both left and right. Essig had turned right, but when Janssen got to the junction he could see no sign of the man. He went right himself, and moved along cautiously, peering into entrances and doorways, but somehow his quarry had escaped him. Essig had simply disappeared into the night.

Janssen retraced his steps, then he cowered down in a dark archway himself, and waited. Essig would soon emerge from wherever he was hiding, he thought. But when more than ten minutes had elapsed, he got up again and left the area, feeling terribly stupid. But still, he had the laptop, and that was important.

When he was almost back at his hotel, he called Lyons on his mobile phone.

Lyons was pottering about at home. She didn't feel like cooking, so she was waiting for Hays to arrive before ordering a takeaway for them both. Just as she heard Hays' key in the front door, her phone rang.

Janssen gave her the details of what had transpired, and apologised for the fact that he had managed to lose Essig so easily.

"I am usually better than that, I promise," he said rather sheepishly.

"We'd better come and meet you. Try not to handle the PC. Where are you now?" she said.

"I'm just arriving back at the hotel – the Imperial."

"OK. Well, wait there for us, we'll be along in about twenty minutes."

"What's up?" Hays said when he heard the tail end of the conversation.

"Our Dutchman has gone rogue and tried to solve the whole bloody thing on his own. But at least he managed to get what we believe is Geller's PC. C'mon, I'll explain all in the car."

* * *

Peadar Tobin was quite enjoying his new role as undercover Lothario. He had called into the Eurosaver shop in Westport after leaving Lyons, and spent a good twenty minutes chatting up Rami, whom he didn't find particularly attractive, but she seemed flattered by the attention he was giving her, and before he left the shop he had an arrangement to meet her for a drink at eight thirty after the shop had closed for the night.

She had given him her address, which turned out to be a rather ramshackle house at the edge of town, but when she appeared in response to his ring on the bell, he was pleasantly surprised. The rather dowdy and poorly dressed shop girl he had been talking to earlier was transformed into a very pretty young woman. She had clearly washed and styled her mousy brown hair, so that it now fell in gentle waves to her shoulders, and she had put on a very subtle layer of makeup and done her eyes too. She was dressed in stylish clothes, which, although not expensive, showed off her shapely figure to good effect. Tobin was going to enjoy this!

Pretending to be a visiting businessman, Tobin asked Rami to suggest a place they could go for a drink, and maybe something to eat, and Rami steered them both to The Fiddlers – a pub that served food late into the evening.

Tobin spent the first hour of their date asking Rami all about herself, her family and her circumstances back home. She seemed to enjoy talking about herself, and by the time she had quaffed a third glass of white wine, it was clear that her inhibitions were evaporating. She was becoming quite flirtatious, and Tobin responded in kind. But ever mindful of his main task, he gently and unobtrusively turned the conversation to Rami's work, and her employer.

"So what's McCutcheon like to work for?" he said.

"That's all depends," she said, her twinkling eyes full of mischief.

"Oh yes. How's that?"

"Well, if you agree to meet him after work for 'stock-taking', he can be quite generous, so I've been told."

"Really? Have you ever done any stock-taking with him?"

"Not likely. He's repulsive. Even though a girl has needs," she said, putting her hand on Tobin's knee under the table, "but really – there are limits."

"So who has been with him then? And where do they go?"

"Ineke is his favourite. She goes with him once or twice a week and gets some nice presents. He gave her a tiny bar of gold last month. And I think he has a place down by the Quay – a small warehouse with living rooms, Ineke says."

"Really? Quite an operator then. Is that the main warehouse for the shop?" Tobin said.

"No, we have big shed round the back of shop. I don't know what he keeps in other one. But sometimes when we get boxes of stuff from China, he takes some and says he's going to the other store. Weird really," Rami said.

"Yes, indeed it is. Have you ever been to the other store?"

"No. I just work in the shop. Anyway, can we get some food? I'm starving."

"Yes, of course. Order what you like – my treat," Tobin replied.

It was after 2 a.m. when Peadar Tobin left the rather down at heel house on the edge of Westport to drive back to Clifden, leaving Rami sound asleep.

"I'd better not call the inspector at this hour," he said to himself as he walked towards his car.

Chapter Sixteen

Hays and Lyons arrived at the Imperial Hotel on Eyre Square twenty minutes later. Lyons parked the Volvo out front, and put the Garda sign in the front windscreen as she had previously. They found Janssen in the lounge with the laptop now secure in a clear plastic bag beside him on the bench seat.

"Good evening, Superintendent, Inspector. Can I get you a drink?" Janssen said.

"Thanks, I'd love a pint of Guinness. Maureen?" Hays said.

"A white wine for me please, Luuk."

Janssen summoned the waitress and ordered their drinks.

"Well, you've been busy, Luuk. Tell us what happened," Hays said.

Janssen explained the full circumstances of how he had come by the laptop, and then the way he had intended to follow Essig to find out where he was living, so that the Gardaí could move in and arrest him.

"I would have called you if I had been able to determine his address, I promise. I'm sorry if I messed up."

"Well, never mind that. At least we have the laptop now thanks to your efforts, but what happened to your role as observer?" Lyons said, although you could tell by her tone she wasn't really vexed.

"Yes, I got a bit carried away, I'm afraid. But at least he didn't identify me, and as you say, we have the laptop."

"Just as well the handbills haven't been circulated yet. If they had, he would have vanished by now. I'm going to call Sinéad Loughran and ask her to come over and collect this. If she can get whatever prints and trace evidence there is on it this evening, we can give it to John in the morning and he can get to work on it. I'm sure it's been wiped, but he'll probably be able to get something from it," Lyons said.

"Do you think any of the other lads you met are in any way involved?" Lyons asked Janssen.

"I don't think so. I'm not sure how they know him, but I guess these types stick together when they are in a foreign city."

"Would you be able to identify them again?" Hays said.

"Yes. For sure. And we might be able to get their prints, if I went back to that pub and asked the barman for their empty bottles. They were all drinking without glasses," Janssen said.

"No, I don't think so, Luuk. Let's leave it to us now, if you don't mind. We appreciate your willingness to help, but we have to be careful with how we obtain evidence. Anyway, you say you don't think they are involved," Lyons said.

"Yes, you are right. Sorry, I was just trying to help."

"And you have been a great help so far, Luuk. We wouldn't have been able to identify Essig without you. And we appreciate that, but best to keep out of it. With a bit of luck, we will be able to get to the bottom of this quickly."

Loughran arrived just as Hays and Lyons were finishing their drinks. She took the laptop away saying that she would get to work on it immediately, and that she would be able to hand it over to O'Connor in the morning.

While Lyons was dealing with Loughran, Hays was on the phone to the station instructing uniformed patrols to step up their activity in the town centre. He also told them to stop any Nissan Micras that they saw being driven by a single male, and interrogate the driver. If there were any uniformed Gardaí over, they were to start house-to-house in the area near the pub where Janssen had met Essig, using the handbills to see if anyone knew of his whereabouts. The manhunt was on.

* * *

Hays, Lyons and Janssen had a meal in the hotel, and spent a couple of hours discussing police work in general, and how important links across Europe now were in solving many different types of crime.

"With cheap air fares, and the internet, it's very easy for criminals to move around Europe these days. They can commit a serious crime in any European country and be gone within a few hours. It makes things very difficult for us," Janssen said.

"Do you have much luck hacking into their systems?" Lyons asked between mouthfuls of roast beef.

"Yes, we do. Even in Utrecht we have a team of twelve technologists who have some good success, and the phone companies and internet providers are quite a good help too. Then in Amsterdam, at headquarters, there is a much bigger team that deals with a lot of the international stuff. But mostly we only catch the more stupid ones that way. The clever ones are often ahead of us, unfortunately. How do you manage here in Galway?" Janssen said.

"Garda John O'Connor," Hays said.

"What about him?" Janssen replied.

"That's it. He's our techy department. But to be fair, up to very recently, policing in Galway has been done very differently than on the mainland of Europe. Here, we have a lot of small Garda stations located all over the country. The local police know what is going on in their area, and generally keep things well under control. But it is changing. I sit on a Technology Committee for the police, and we have close contact with the UK who are a good bit further ahead than we are. We are slowly getting up to date, but the problem I have is that the people at the very top of our structure don't really understand technology. They are more used to typewriters and landlines, so it can be a struggle," Hays said.

The three continued their chat until the meal was over, and then Hays and Lyons departed for home having arranged for Janssen to meet them in Mill Street at eight o'clock in the morning.

* * *

The following day it was all systems go at Mill Street station. Peadar Tobin was on the phone to Lyons giving details of what he had learned from Rami the previous night.

"That's great, Peadar. Well done. Have you arranged to see her again?" Lyons said.

"No, boss. I told her I was just passing through and left it loose. But I could if you wanted me to."

"No, leave it for now. But I want you to find out from the boys in Westport exactly where McCutcheon's other warehouse is. We might be able to arrange a surprise visit and catch him with his pants down – literally!" Lyons said.

"I see what you mean. Right, I'll get on to that straight away and let you know."

"But, Peadar, be very discreet. Word has a habit of leaking out over these things, and if McCutcheon thinks we're onto him, he'll close everything down. He's no eejit."

"Don't worry, boss. I'm good friends with one or two of the lads from Westport. I'll make sure it's kept nice and tight."

"Great. Thanks. Talk soon," Lyons said.

Sinéad Loughran had brought the stolen PC across to John O'Connor by the time Lyons was off the phone.

"Hi, Sinéad," Lyons said, "thanks for bringing that over. Did you get anything off it?"

"It's definitely Geller's. I got her fingerprints off the side of the keyboard. The outside had been wiped, but not very well. Oh, and I noticed there's an SD card still stuck in it too. Maybe John will be able to get something from that."

"That's great, Sinéad, thanks. What about other dabs?"

"Just a few smudges I'm afraid, but didn't Liam Walsh and Mary Costelloe see the victim with it in his possession?"

"Yes, you're right, they did. And Liam had the presence of mind to note down the serial number too, so that's pretty conclusive. Now all we need to do is to find Essig. We're fairly sure he killed both victims, but we're not sure exactly why," Lyons said.

"Good luck with that. OK, well, if you don't need me for anything else, I'll be off. Call me anytime, Maureen."

"Thanks, Sinéad."

As Loughran was leaving the office, Hays loomed up in the doorway.

"Hi. We're wanted upstairs. It's Plunkett, and he doesn't sound happy!"

* * *

"Come," boomed Chief Superintendent Finbarr Plunkett's voice from the other side of the door when Lyons knocked. She glanced back at her partner and rolled her eyes to heaven, and then went in.

Plunkett said nothing as the two entered and approached his desk.

"Sit," the man instructed, and the two detectives obeyed silently.

"What in the name of all that's wonderful is going on, you two?" Plunkett said.

"Sorry, sir, what do you mean?" Hays said.

"Don't get cute with me, Mick, you know full well what I'm talking about. You seem to have recruited some foreign policeman to do your dirty work for you. You know bloody well any half decent defence barrister will tear the arse out of us for that. What's going on?" Plunkett said, his face red with rage as he spoke.

"Look. We have two murders on our hands here, sir. As far as we can ascertain, there is some connection to a gang operating some kind of scam that involves eastern Europe, the Netherlands and even China. Inspector

Janssen is from Utrecht which seems to be a hub for them. He came over as an observer, and he's been very helpful in identifying the man we think killed these two people. So we're indebted to him for that," Hays said.

"I heard he was out doing some undercover work for you. Is that correct, and don't even think of bull-shitting me, Mick."

"No, sir, that's not correct." And Hays went on to explain how Janssen had come by the laptop, but making the story a little more vague than the reality of the situation.

"So, your most junior officer has basically saved your skin by taking down the serial number. Is that what you're telling me?" Plunkett said, refusing to be placated.

"It's been a team effort, sir," Lyons said rather tentatively.

"And what's been your part in all of this, Inspector Lyons?"

"As Superintendent Hays said, sir, it's been a real team effort. Everyone has played an important role. And I think we may have an opportunity to crack open a pretty nasty smuggling and tax avoidance operation that has some local connections too, given the chance," Lyons said.

"What do you mean? Don't you know this fella has full operational control for the region?" Plunkett said, nodding at Hays. "Who's involved in this scam of yours anyway? And this better be good!"

"We're still collecting evidence, sir, but we believe there may be a Westport connection. In fact, we will be applying for a warrant to search premises out there," Lyons said.

"Look," Plunkett said, calming down a little. "You two have a good track record. But whatever you're up to, you'd better make damn sure it doesn't end coming back to bite us. If you're going to make waves all over the bloody west of Ireland with your scams and schemes, it'd better be tight. Tight as a duck's back-side – and that's watertight! Do I make myself clear?" Plunkett said.

"Yes, sir, of course, sir," Hays said.

"Good. And I don't want to hear any more about this Dutchman of yours either. Keep him out of it, OK?"

"Yes, sir. Will that be all, sir?" Hays said.

"Inspector, you can go. Mick, will you hang on for a minute please?"

Lyons got up and left the room, knowing that the two men would be talking about her as soon as she was gone, but she had more sense than to try and listen at the door.

"Was I too hard on her, Mick?" Plunkett asked when Lyons had left.

"This is a bitch of a case, Finbarr. She's doing OK on it, and the rest of the team are right behind her. I think she'll bring it in OK, but it will take a bit more time, and to be honest, there may be some flak flying before it's all over. Your man in Westport is probably well connected, so when she moves in on him there could be a bit of turbulence. But I'll be keeping an eye out, don't worry."

"Jaysus, Mick – don't let her go feral on us. She's gone out on a limb a few times before, and this bloody thing could have international repercussions. It won't do either of us any good if we come unstuck."

"To be fair, she's got some very good results in the past. I know her style is all her own, but somehow it all seems to work out in the end," Hays said.

"Let's hope so, Mick, let's hope so. Be sure to keep me informed, won't you?"

"Of course. Will you sort out that warrant for us?"

"Ah, look after that yourself, Mick. I don't want to be too close to it in case it all goes pear shaped. That way I can step in and defend you if I haven't been involved."

"OK. I'll sort it. I'd best get on."

Chapter Seventeen

As the efforts of the local Gardaí intensified in Galway, out in Clifden and in Westport, several reported sightings of Dieter Essig came into the control room. Each one had to be followed up, which was time consuming, and generally fruitless. But half way through the afternoon, the Gardaí got a call from a Teresa Birchall, the owner of a small jewellery shop in the heart of the city. Birchall was known to the Gardaí, and not for any good reasons. They suspected that she was fencing stolen property from time to time, but she had been clever enough to avoid prosecution so far, so when they took the call, the Gardaí were a bit surprised.

Birchall told them that a man had come into the shop just after lunch with some gold to sell. That wasn't unusual in itself, but this time Teresa felt there was something a bit iffy about the guy, so, pretending that she was not the boss, told the man that she would have to get the merchandise valued by the owner, asking him to call back later.

They arranged that he would come back after 4 p.m. at which time she would have an offer for him, and she told him it would be the best offer available based on current prices, which seemed to satisfy him. When the man had left the shop, she looked at the handbill that the Gardaí had left there during the morning, and she was reasonably sure that it was the same bloke.

Flynn and Lyons got together as soon as the call had been logged. There was a lot to arrange.

"Who's firearms trained?" Flynn asked.

"There's you and me for starters, and I think Sally has permission now too. Ask her, and then arrange for us to draw as many firearms as we have authorized officers. We'll have to arrange a stake out, and we haven't much time. Keep Liam and Mary out of it in case he may have seen them at some stage," Lyons said.

Flynn left the office to make the arrangements and Lyons called Hays to put him in the picture.

"Bloody hell, Maureen, be very careful love. If this guy is armed, we can't have a shoot-out in the middle of town. Anyone could get hurt, and you can just imagine what Plunkett would have to say about that!"

"Don't worry, Mick. I have a plan."

"God help us all – don't tell me – he's going to get Maureened," Hays said.

"Something like that. And I'll try not to kill too many bystanders!"

* * *

Birchalls was a small single-fronted shop located in a narrow street off the main shopping area in the centre of Galway. The lane it was on led down to the docks where there was a large car park, so the shop enjoyed a good footfall, though many of the pedestrians passed it by, hurrying back to their vehicles. Nevertheless, it managed a good level of trade for its size, and the owner, Teresa Birchall, was well known and well liked among the business community.

To the side of the shop there was a very narrow alley that was used for access and storing bins, and the shop had a rear door that opened onto it, although this was only used by the staff.

The window onto the street was brightly lit with spotlights making the various engagement rings and other glittering jewels sparkle, and there was a good selection of brand named watches for both ladies and gents, as well as a generous tray of Claddagh rings in a number of styles and sizes on display as well.

Inside the shop, which was quite small, there were a number of slim display cabinets lining the walls, and a serve-over counter with a glass top covering a further selection of trinkets.

The detectives arrived at the premises at fifteen minutes before four o'clock. They had rather hurriedly withdrawn firearms from the armoury at the station, and Flynn, Fahy and Lyons now each had a SIG Sauer 9mm pistol concealed beneath their jackets.

The plan was for Flynn to assume the role of the owner of the shop, and to face Dieter Essig across the counter. He would look for an opportunity to surprise the man, and see if he could effect an arrest without using his weapon. Lyons and Fahy would remain outside. Lyons would stand at the corner of the little alleyway, so that she could cover both the main door and the rear exit, just in case. Fahy would pretend to be window shopping, and would observe the goings-on inside the shop through the glass. When Essig arrived, they were both to draw their weapons and keep them discreetly by their side, ready for action if necessary.

Fortunately, it was a fine afternoon in Galway. There was quite a stiff breeze that whistled down the narrow street, but with high, thin, patchy clouds, there was a good deal of sunshine too, although not much of it penetrated the site of Birchall's shop, due to the narrowness of the street and the height of the surrounding buildings.

Essig arrived soon after four o'clock and entered the shop, where another customer was having a new battery fitted to her watch. He waited for Teresa to finish the task, and her conversation with the customer whom she appeared to know, before approaching the counter. The woman left the shop, totally unaware of the drama that was about to unfold.

"You have my money?" Essig asked Teresa Birchall.

"Oh, yes. I'll just get the owner for you, he has valued it now."

On cue, Flynn emerged from the back of the shop which was screened off, looking dapper in a suit, shirt and tie, the latter borrowed from a colleague at Mill Street at the last minute.

"Yes, sir," I have your merchandise here, just under the counter. Flynn reached below the glass worktop and came up with his pistol pointing straight at Essig.

Essig was quick. He screamed out loud, and in the split second as Flynn and Birchall were distracted, he whipped out his own gun and pointed it at the shopkeeper.

"I will shoot her. Believe me, I have nothing to lose. Now put down your weapon and give me the money, and I'll go. Quick!" he barked.

Flynn had no intention of doing anything of the kind.

"If you shoot anyone in here, you will be dead within two seconds. There are armed officers all around this building, and you won't get away, I promise you," he said coolly. He had however placed his own gun on the counter in case Essig would shoot the woman in cold blood.

"Here," Essig said, waving his weapon at the woman. "You're with me. Come out!"

Teresa Birchall was terrified. So much so, that her legs wouldn't move – she was frozen to the spot with fear.

Essig leaned across the counter, and keeping the gun pointed at Teresa Birchall's chest, grabbed her by the hair and started to pull her around the side of the counter.

Fahy, who had seen the entire performance from her viewpoint on the pavement, decided that it was time for action. Raising her gun to waist level, she crashed in through the shop door shouting, "Down, everyone down!"

Essig didn't know which way to turn, but his eyes had gone wild, and the Gardaí realised that he could start shooting at any moment, and could easily kill both Flynn and the shop owner before they could retaliate. But Fahy wasn't finished yet. Taking careful aim, she fired a single shot into the man's knee. He dropped like a stone onto the carpeted floor, blood oozing out from a wide wound in his torn trousers. At the same time, the arm in which he was holding his gun came up, and he fired a shot, but it was a futile gesture, as the bullet went harmlessly up into the ceiling tiles.

Fahy was now standing over the man with her pistol pointed at his head.

"Give me a reason," she said. "Just flinch, and you're a dead man."

Lyons had come into the shop behind Fahy, and quickly stepped over to take Essig's gun and make it safe, putting her own pistol away too.

Flynn was on the phone, calling for an ambulance. Mrs Birchall was propped up against the shop counter, sobbing uncontrollably. When Lyons had disarmed Essig, she went over to her and started to console the woman.

"It's all over now, Teresa. Don't worry, you're fine, and you did very well. And look on the bright side – this will do your business no harm at all when it gets into the papers. They'll be queueing down the street to come in and buy something."

At this, the woman gave a nervous giggle. Lyons recognised that Teresa Birchall was in shock, and gently led her to the back of the shop where there was a rudimentary kitchen. Lyons made two mugs of strong sugary tea, and sat Teresa down to drink it.

The ambulance arrived at the end of the narrow street and two paramedics jogged down to the shop. Fahy recognised the girl in the green uniform.

"Hi, Jane. This one has taken a bullet to his knee, but I don't think it's too serious. Can you patch him up as quick as you can? We need to interview him. And don't be too gentle with him," Fahy said.

The paramedics started working on Essig, cutting away his shredded pants, and tending to the wound which by now had almost stopped bleeding. Fahy's aim had been good, the damage was quite modest, but the leg probably very sore.

"The bullet went straight through, Sally. We'll bandage him up and give him an anti-tetanus jab and a few Paracetamol and he'll be grand. He won't be playing football for a week or two though," Jane said.

"Don't worry about that. He won't be playing football where he's going anyway."

Lyons arranged for a Garda car to take Teresa Birchall home when she had finished her tea. She was recovering slowly from the ordeal, and thanked Lyons for her consideration, asking that the shop be well secured before they left, and handing over the alarm codes.

"Don't worry, Teresa, we'll make sure it's well locked up. We just need to take a good few photographs, as a firearm has been discharged. Sorry about the carpet. Maybe tomorrow, if you're feeling up to it, you could come in to Mill Street and make a statement?" Lyons said.

"Yes, of course. I'll get Gerard to open up here, and I'll drop down at about ten-thirty."

"Perfect. And if I may ask, be careful what you say to the media – you know what they are like – this is all part of a bigger enquiry involving some pretty nasty stuff," Lyons said.

"Yes, OK. I'll just stick to what I know, if it arises, and thanks again, you were great, all of you."

* * *

It was nearly seven o'clock when Lyons, Flynn and Fahy got back to the station. They found Hays chatting to Janssen in the open plan office. Mary Costelloe, Liam Walsh and John O'Connor were there too talking amongst themselves.

Hays stood up when he saw the team arriving.

"Well done, everybody. A great result. Come in and tell us all about it."

The three detectives told the story without elaboration, each of them contributing their own element so that no detail was left out. When they had finished, Lyons took the floor.

"That's about it, folks, and I'm sorry to put a damper on the euphoria, but we're a long way from getting a conviction. We still can't tie Essig to Maria Geller's murder, or the other guy either. So we have a lot more to do. But I will say it was thanks to Sally's quick thinking, and even quicker response that the situation at the jewellers was resolved without loss of life. If she hadn't acted when she did, quite possibly Teresa Birchall would have been shot dead, so well done, Sally. Now, you take your gun and the spent shell back to the armoury and start the paperwork. Sinéad will get Essig's bullet out of the ceiling tomorrow when she's down there doing her forensic bit."

Fahy and Flynn left the room to go and check in their weapons. Fahy would have to write a very detailed report on the discharge of her firearm, and the sooner she got started on it the better.

When they had gone, Hays said, "I might see if we can get a commendation for Fahy out of this. She was very brave, and showed damn fine judgement, if you ask me."

"I agree, Mick. Good idea," Lyons said.

"Right, well, what next?" Hays asked.

"Now we start trying to put the whole thing together. We'll have to see what forensic evidence we can get against Essig. We will also have to see if he's prepared to talk at all about what's going on, but we'll leave him in the cells for tonight. I'll start interviewing him in the morning with Eamon," Lyons said.

"I wonder if I could be of any help?" Janssen asked.

"Let me think about that overnight, Luuk. I'd like to get you involved if we can, but just now I'm not quite sure how. But I'll think of something, don't worry," Lyons said.

"If I were you, Luuk, I'd be very worried indeed. This officer has something of a reputation for unconventional policing, so watch out," Hays said with a big smile.

On the way home, alone in her car, Lyons called Peadar Tobin on his mobile.

"Hello," he said.

"Peadar, it's Maureen Lyons. Look, is there any chance you could arrange another date with your friend from Westport – Rami, was it?"

"Hmmm, probably. What's up?"

"I need to know when McCutcheon has his next romantic liaison arranged with his little Dutch friend. And obviously we can't ask Ineke or McCutcheon. Do you think you can find out for me?" Lyons said.

"I'd say so. I'll call her and see if she's free for a drink later on and I'll drive over."

"Great, thanks Peadar, but for heaven's sake, don't get caught out."

"Don't worry on that score, Inspector, I'll be very careful," Tobin said.

"Right. Oh, and let me know at once if you find anything out. Thanks."

Chapter Eighteen

The following morning, before Lyons went down to the interview room to start discussions with Dieter Essig, she cornered John O'Connor as he arrived for work.

"John, did you get anything from the phone or the laptop?"

"I sure did, boss. Lots in fact. I'm nearly finished writing it up in the system, but there are texts and emails between Geller and Essig going back a good while, and though they don't mention gold specifically, it's pretty clear that's what is being referred to."

"Excellent. Any evidence that they had a meeting arranged for the night she was killed?" Lyons asked.

"Not quite that specific, but there is an email from Essig that says 'See you at 22 at nine o'clock. Have goods with you'."

"That'll do me. Make sure all that evidence is secured. Did Sinéad get anything from the gold that we brought back in from the jewellers last night?"

"I'm not sure, boss. She's gone back out there this morning. Would you like me to call her?" O'Connor said.

"Yes, please. You know what we're looking for – fingerprints or any other trace evidence that can link it to Geller. I think I'm beginning to figure out what happened, but we'll see."

As Lyons went to leave the room, Janssen walked in.

"Hi, Luuk. Listen, I do want your help this morning. If you could just wait here for a while, I'll call you down to join the interview, and when you come into the room, just follow my lead. OK?"

Lyons had decided to start the interview on her own with Essig. Of course, the duty solicitor would be present, and a uniformed Garda, but she didn't want to bring in any of the other detectives for the moment. She grabbed a coffee on the way downstairs, and entered the room where Essig was seated alongside a young man in a suit whom she took to be the solicitor.

When all the introduction had been completed, the duty solicitor asked, "What exactly are you intending to charge my client with, Inspector?"

"It's a bit soon for that, Mr Mulvaney. We will have to see how this interview goes, and if your client is prepared to co-operate with us."

"And what is it that you think he can help you with?" Mulvaney asked.

"We have a number of charges that we are considering. They include robbery; assault; illegal possession of a firearm; attempted murder of a police officer, and quite possibly two counts of actual murder."

Mulvaney raised his eyebrows and made some notes on his jotter. Essig remained silent with a contemptuous look on his face.

"And I assume you have evidence to back up these allegations, Inspector," the solicitor said.

"Look, why don't you stop fishing Mr Mulvaney, and let me get on with doing my job. Otherwise we'll be here all day!"

Lyons started by asking where Essig was on the night Maria Geller had been murdered. He made no response, so Lyons went on to say that they had evidence that he had arranged to meet the woman on the night she was killed at nine o'clock. Still, there was no response of any kind from the suspect.

She then turned her attention to the gold, asking how he had come into possession of the hoard that he had left at the jeweller's shop to have valued with a view to a sale.

"My client denies ever being in possession of any gold, Inspector. Unless you can prove it, this is all fabrication," Mulvaney said.

"I have his fingerprints all over a number of gold items, and I have a witness statement identifying your client as the man who brought a consignment of the stuff into her shop with the intention of selling it to her. I also have the actual gold itself, and my forensic team are at this moment working to establish if this is part of the same haul that was found in Maria Geller's house after she was murdered," Lyons said.

Neither man made any reply, so Lyons went on.

"And if I were in your shoes, Mr Mulvaney, I would advise my client to start co-operating with this enquiry immediately in the hope that it might in some way mitigate the very serious circumstances in which he finds himself."

Again, both men remained silent.

Lyons tried a few different approaches to get Essig to open up, but none of it had any effect. He remained stoically silent with the same glum look on his face, and the only response she could get from either of them was the occasional interruption from the solicitor challenging some assertion she had made. After a further forty minutes, she decided to switch things around and left the room.

Fahy and Flynn were next to have a go at loosening the tongue of the recalcitrant Essig.

When Fahy entered the interview room, she asked Essig how his knee was, and if it was still very painful. He simply grunted. When he saw Flynn though, the reaction was different. He whispered in Mulvaney's ear, and the solicitor immediately spoke up.

"My client tells me that Inspector Flynn here was impersonating the owner of a jewellery shop yesterday afternoon. You do realise, I suppose, that that is grounds for entrapment," he said coolly.

"Just as well I was there," Flynn said, "otherwise he would almost certainly have killed the woman behind the counter in an effort to escape captivity."

Fahy leaned in across the table and looked Essig straight in the eyes.

"Why don't you tell us all about it, Dieter. We know that this is all being run by some eastern European mob. We know you are only a small player – very dispensable. They won't think anything of sacrificing you to twenty or more years in jail here. Or maybe worse. So, now would be a good time to help yourself by helping us. Who is behind your gold smuggling scheme?"

Essig said nothing, but returned Fahy's look with a fierce contempt. He then spat at her, leaving a trail of sputum slowly running down her cheek.

Fahy took a tissue from her pocket and wiped it away.

"That's another charge we can add to the sheet, and this is a good one, because it has been witnessed by an officer of the court as well as another police officer – isn't that right, Mr Mulvaney?" she said.

"You clearly provoked him, Sergeant. What did you expect?" Mulvaney said.

"Well, it's the least of his worries. Does the name Matis Vitkus mean anything to you, Mr Essig?" Fahy said.

There was no response from the suspect, but Fahy noticed his eyes flare a little – a sure sign that he had recognised the name.

"Who is this person, Sergeant, and what connection does he have to my client?"

"At this very moment, our forensic team is matching the bullet that killed Mr Vitkus to the gun we removed from your client in the jeweller's shop yesterday afternoon. We will find your client's prints on the shell casing recovered from Vitkus' bedsit room, giving us proof that your client murdered Vitkus, possibly because he thought Vitkus had gone to the police, or was being careless with some stolen property."

"That is all conjecture. I've never heard such wild unsubstantiated accusations. Really, Sergeant, if you are not going to charge my client, I must insist you release him at once," Mulvaney protested.

"Oh, but we are going to charge him, Mr Mulvaney. But you'll have to be patient a little longer. Would you and your client like a comfort break?" Flynn said.

* * *

Sinéad Loughran had left two of her team at Birchall's shop, and had returned to her lab close to Mill Street Garda Station. She had supervised the matching of the bullet from Essig's gun to the one that was retrieved from Vitkus' room. She was happy that the match would stand up in court, and she passed the information on to Lyons as soon as she could.

Now that they had a clear set of fingerprints from Dieter Essig, they could compare them to prints and partial prints that they had been able to recover from various items connected to the murder of Maria Geller. It would take time, but Loughran was sure that they would come up with something useful.

Lyons had a short chat with Luuk Janssen who was waiting patiently in the open plan area, and the two of them headed back down to the interview room where Essig and his solicitor had been provided with coffee.

Lyons and her companion entered the room, and took their seats opposite Essig.

"Mr Essig, allow me to introduce Special Investigating Agent, Luuk Janssen. Mr Janssen is from Europe, and has been sent over to assist us with this matter. You may recognise him – he was the man who purchased the stolen laptop from you in the pub the other day," Lyons said.

"Really, Inspector, I must protest. This is highly irregular. What jurisdiction has Mr Janssen got?" Mulvaney said.

"Don't worry on that score, Mr Mulvaney. Mr Janssen is here on the highest authority, believe me."

Janssen then began to speak.

"Mr Essig. We have been following your progress for some time now, and I can assure you, with the help of the Gardaí, we have enough evidence against you to put you away for a very long time indeed. And even after you are released from Irish custody, after many years, you will be deported to Europe where you will serve a lot more years in prison. So, for you, Mr Essig, the game, as they say, is up."

Janssen paused to let the significance of what he had said sink in before continuing.

"Of course, there are some among the higher ranks here in Ireland who would rather not prosecute you. They don't like spending lots of money keeping people in prison who should rightly be incarcerated in other countries, and after all none of your victims are Irish. It has been suggested that it might be easier for all concerned if you were to be deported, without charge here in Ireland. Romania has been suggested, where I believe you have certain contacts already. But of course, before you go back there, we would advise your connections of the tremendous assistance you had provided to the Irish and international police with names and locations of a number of gang members. We would even round up a few of these men just to make the point."

At this, Essig became very agitated and his eyes were wide with fear.

"You can't do that," he shouted, "it's totally illegal."

Mulvaney shifted uneasily in his seat, but said nothing.

"Not as illegal as some of the things you have been up to, Mr Essig. And besides, once you are back in Romania, you can take the matter up with the European Court of Justice if you believe your rights have been violated," Janssen said.

"European Court – pah! I'll be dead, and you know it. What you say is nothing short of murder!"

"As we say in Ireland, Mr Essig, 'what goes around, comes around'," Lyons said.

Mulvaney could not remain silent any longer.

"Hypothetically, of course, if my client were to provide some information that was of use to the authorities, how might it help him with the current issues?"

"We would have to see what he could tell us, and what it led to. But if we could break this smuggling gang wide open, and put a good few of them behind bars, recover a good amount of the merchandise, we might be able to help him with some of the charges. But first, he needs to tell us all he knows. Otherwise, no deal," Lyons said.

"I need a little time to consult with my client, Inspector. May we say twenty minutes?" Mulvaney said.

"Yes, fine. We'll be back then," she said as the two of them got up and left the room.

"Wow. I see what Superintendent meant by unconventional methods. That was awesome. But what will you do with him after he has told you all he knows?" Janssen asked as they walked back upstairs.

"I was thinking of handing him over into your custody, to be honest. Of course, we would provide all the evidence so that you could try him for murder, and some of us would attend the trial if you needed us. How would that work for you?"

"I would be most grateful. I could take him back to Utrecht where I am sure we can charge him with many things. But what would your superiors say?"

"I'll check with them, but I imagine they would be quite happy with it. We have enough to be doing with our own criminals without getting involved with this lot. But we'll need to close down any local connections here. We don't want this whole thing starting up again after he's gone. Let's see what information he can provide."

Chapter Nineteen

Batty McCutcheon left home just before eight o'clock to go back into Westport.

"I'm just going back to the office for an hour or so, I have to do my emails, and there's no signal out here as usual," he said to his wife.

He drove directly to the secondary store that he kept down by the harbour. Ineke had already let herself in, and was sitting in the large comfortable sitting room above the storeroom, sipping a glass of white wine that she had taken from the well-stocked fridge.

When McCutcheon arrived a few minutes later, they embraced, and then he too went to get himself a drink. They sat and exchanged small talk for five minutes on the sofa, and then McCutcheon took the girl by the hand and led her to the bedroom, where a comfortable double bed was positioned opposite the window with a magnificent view out over the sea. The two undressed each other slowly, kissing and stroking as they did so, and soon they were both naked between the sheets.

"Go, go, go," Flynn shouted into the radio he was holding, and Liam Walsh, Mary Costelloe and three uniformed Gardaí descended on the building, the lead officer pounding on the door.

After thirty seconds there was no response, so the door was kicked in, and the entire party scrambled up the stairs.

Flynn was the first to arrive in the bedroom where McCutcheon and his lover were sitting up holding the bedsheet in front of their nakedness.

"What the fuck! Who the hell are you, and what are you doing here?" McCutcheon shouted at Flynn.

"My name is Inspector Eamon Flynn from Galway Gardaí, and I have a warrant to search this entire premises. Please put some clothes on. My colleague Garda Costelloe will stay with the girl."

"By Christ, I hope you'll enjoy walking the beat out on the Aran Islands, Flynn, by the time I'm finished with you," McCutcheon ranted, grabbing his underpants and struggling into them.

The uniformed Gardaí were busy making a methodical search of the store beneath McCutcheon's love nest. They were recording the whole thing on various phones, and going through each of the boxes one by one, most of which had Chinese symbols in black stencil on the outside.

After twenty minutes or so one of the uniformed officers let out a shout.

"Sir, down here, sir. I've got something."

Flynn heard the call and went down to the storeroom which was now in some disarray with opened cartons all over the place.

"Yes, what is it?" he said to the excited young Garda who was holding a package of what looked like tea towels in his hand.

"Here, sir. Look. Beneath the towels, there's a tray of small gold bars. There's thirty of them in this lot alone."

"Right. Good work. Bag it up, tea towels and all, and keep looking, there may be a lot more."

Upstairs, another uniformed officer was disassembling McCutcheon's computer. He separated the keyboard, monitor and mouse from each other and placed each component into a large clear plastic bag.

"You can't take that. That's my private stuff. I need it for my business," growled McCutcheon. The young Garda ignored McCutcheon's protestations and continued bagging up files and papers.

In the bedroom, Mary Costelloe was trying to console the poor Dutch girl, who was now fully clothed but in a very distressed state.

"It's OK, Ineke, you've done nothing wrong. Don't worry, it will be fine," Costelloe said, with her arm around the girl's shoulders.

By the time the search had been completed, ten trays of thirty gold ingots each had been recovered. They were in varying sizes, but represented many thousands of euros worth of the precious metal.

Flynn approached McCutcheon, who had gone uncharacteristically quiet.

"I presume you can provide customs papers and VAT receipts for this lot, Mr McCutcheon." But there was no reply.

McCutcheon was handcuffed and taken away to Westport Garda Station where he was booked in, the desk sergeant being told that serious charges were likely to follow. The belt from his trousers and his shoe laces were removed, and he was shown to a cold, rather damp and none too clean cell for the night.

Flynn thanked the Gardaí for their help, and asked Mary Costelloe to see Ineke to her home. Walsh was to go with Flynn to see Mrs McCutcheon who by now must surely have been wondering where her husband had got to.

"How do you want to play this, sir?" Walsh asked as they drove out to the McCutcheon house.

"Just follow my lead, Liam. But if you get the chance, have a snoop around. He has a laptop at home, and if we see it, we might persuade the missus to let us have it, although his house isn't covered by the warrant, so we can't just take it without permission."

"Right, boss. I'll see what I can do."

* * *

Eleanor McCutcheon opened the door, expecting to find her husband on the doorstep having left his house keys at home again.

"Yes, can I help you?" Mrs McCutcheon said with a concerned look on her face.

Flynn introduced them both, and Eleanor McCutcheon immediately jumped to the conclusion that her husband had been involved in an accident.

"No, it's nothing like that, Mrs McCutcheon. May we come in, please?" Flynn said.

"Sorry, yes of course. Please, go through to the kitchen," she said and stood aside to let them pass.

"Your husband is quite safe, Mrs McCutcheon. In fact, we have him in custody," Flynn said.

"In custody? God, I suppose he was caught drink driving. I've warned him before about that, but of course he takes no notice of me."

"No, it's nothing like that. We arrested your husband at his storage depot down at the harbour in the town. He was upstairs, and I'm afraid to say he wasn't alone."

"What storage depot? He hasn't got a warehouse down at the harbour. It must be someone else you've taken in."

Flynn and Walsh exchanged glances.

"I'm afraid there is no mistake. I have met your husband here at the house. It's definitely him, and he's given us his name in any case."

"Not alone, you say. So who was he with then? That mad eejit that manages the shop, I suppose."

"No, in fact it was a young woman, and they were, how shall I put it, not fully clothed when we arrived. In fact they were in bed together."

"What! What are you saying? What girl? This is all nonsense, Batty doesn't have any girl. Are you sure you're not mistaken?"

"Certain, I'm afraid. Listen, could you get someone to come over maybe, stay with you? This has obviously been a terrible shock. I didn't realise you knew nothing about it."

The distraught woman sat down at the kitchen table and took a tissue from her pocket to wipe her streaming eyes. She shook her head slightly from side to side.

"I'm all right. There's no one near in any case. My sister lives in Dublin."

They all remained silent for some minutes and then Mrs McCutcheon asked, "So, what did you arrest him for, anyway, unless the girl was a hooker!"

"No, nothing like that. The girl works in the shop in the town. No, we arrested him for VAT fraud and smuggling, although there may be other charges to follow. We discovered quite a large quantity of Chinese gold on his premises, and we believe he may be involved in some other related business too," Flynn said.

"Chinese gold! God, I've heard it all now. Listen, Mr Flynn, are you sure this isn't some kind of dreadful mix up? My husband isn't that kind of man at all. He's not – really."

"Everything we have told you so far is true, I'm afraid, Mrs McCutcheon. But I really think you should have some company tonight. Would you like me to arrange something?"

"Do what you like. I don't care. It's not going to make it all go away, is it? God, I feel as if I'm in a dream, or a nightmare, more like it."

Flynn signalled to Walsh to go and get Mary Costelloe out to the house with just a simple nod of his head, and the junior officer walked out of earshot to make the call.

"We'll have Mary stay with you tonight, Mrs McCutcheon. Then, if you want to, she can bring you in to Westport tomorrow morning to see your husband. Does he have a solicitor, do you know?"

"Eh, I think so. Some smarmy streak of misery from the town. O'Donnell I think his name is. I never liked him."

"Thanks. We'll contact him later on. Can I ask if your husband's laptop computer is here, Mrs McCutcheon?"

"Yes, it's over on the sofa. He has another one in town, I think."

"Would you mind if we borrowed it? There may be some useful information on it."

"No, go ahead. You can keep it for all I care. Bloody thing doesn't work out here anyway."

Flynn and Walsh waited for Mary Costelloe to arrive at the house. Walsh briefed her before she went inside, and asked her to record anything relevant that Mrs McCutcheon might let slip about her husband and in particular his business arrangements.

"Are we going to caution her?" Costelloe asked.

"No, we'll keep it informal for now. She's very shocked, so just keep her calm and listen to whatever she has to say."

When Liam Walsh and Eamon Flynn had left the McCutcheon house, they called in to Westport Garda station. They got the number for Cecil O'Donnell from the desk sergeant, and telephoned him to advise him that his client was in custody, but that there would be no interview until the morning. O'Donnell was emotionless on hearing the news, and simply asked Flynn to ensure that there would be no questioning of his client until he was in attendance.

Chapter Twenty

The following morning the team held a full briefing, bringing everyone up to date on the find out in Westport, and the fact that Batty McCutcheon was now in custody.

Mary Costelloe had spent the night with Mrs McCutcheon. The woman was now a lot calmer, but her initial disbelief had turned to anger. She wanted to do damage to her husband for his infidelity and for the trouble he had brought down on them, but she didn't know how. It was clear that she knew nothing of his nefarious dealings.

McCutcheon's computer was given to John O'Connor along with the laptop that Flynn had borrowed from the house. O'Connor relished the thought of having two machines to explore, and asked to be excused from the rest of the briefing to get on with it.

Westport Gardaí sent a van down to the harbour to take away all the cartons from the store for safe keeping. When the load was back at the station, the desk sergeant – a wily old timer – summoned the owner of the nearby

Chinese takeaway to help them decipher the writing on the sides of the boxes that would give the Gardaí information about their origin.

Just before ten o'clock, two things happened. Firstly, McCutcheon's solicitor arrived at the Garda station full of bluster, saying that there must be some mistake, his client was an upstanding member of the community and should be released at once with an apology from a senior officer. He was shown into the interview room and told that he had an hour to consult with his client before the formal interview would take place. Detectives from Galway were on their way.

At the same time, Lyons was summoned upstairs to Chief Superintendent Finbarr Plunkett's office. When she arrived on the top floor, she was shown into the office and found her partner, Superintendent Mick Hays, already seated, chatting to the chief.

"Come in Maureen, have a seat. Would you like a coffee or a cup of tea?" Plunkett said. Lyons was used to reading the signals, and knew that if she had been offered refreshments, at least she wasn't in for a bollocking.

"Thanks, sir, yes, a coffee would be lovely." She stole a quick glance at Hays who was smiling back warmly. So far, so good.

"Now, Maureen, I understand you have arrested some foreign bloke for the murder of Maria Geller out in Clifden, is that right?" Plunkett asked.

"Yes, that's right, sir. And we are fairly certain he's responsible for the death of another foreign national as well – a Matis Vitkus. He was shot in a bedsit on Buttermilk Walk."

"So now we have three foreigners all involved in very serious crimes on our patch. Is there any local involvement at all?" Plunkett said.

Maureen went on to explain as briefly as she could how the gold scam was operating. She knew Plunkett had a short attention span, and wouldn't want to be concerned with the detail. When she got to the bit about Batty McCutcheon, Plunkett's interest began to show.

"Now, what about this fella, McCutcheon? How is he tied into all this?"

"We're not sure at the moment, sir. We found a stash of gold bars in one of his warehouses out in Westport, so it looks as if he may have been involved in the distribution end of things. But it's quite complicated. We're working through it now. What's your thinking?"

"Ah, you know how it is, Maureen. All these moguls are connected in some way. Your man has political clout, or at least he thinks he has. He's a contributor to the local party out there and he reckons that gives him license to act the maggot with us. But what have you actually got on him?"

"Well, VAT fraud for sure – and we're talking substantial amounts. And if we can make a connection back to the gold business, and prove that he was a player, then he could be implicated in organised crime," Lyons said.

"Hmm. And what about this Essig chap? What are you planning to do with him?"

"That's more straightforward. I'm sure Sinéad Loughran will be able to tie him back to Geller's killing, and we have him banged to rights for the Vitkus murder, as well as the attempted murder of a serving officer, robbery with menace and a few other things."

Hays could sense the way the senior man was thinking, and decided that this would be a good time to intervene.

"But, Maureen, you see all this is a bit fanciful for us. Sure, crimes have been committed on our patch, but we're not in a position to go chasing down Lithuanian gangs or whatever. That's best left to Europol or the local police out there. What if we were to say that you can have McCutcheon and do your worst? We need to send a message to the likes of him anyway that these small town businessmen can't get away with these kinds of fiddles. But do you think we could get rid of the other bloke, Essig? Find a way of sending him off somewhere, into the custody of some European police force of course, I don't mean let him go. As you know our resources are scarce enough, without trying to solve all of Europe's crimes as well," Hays said.

Lyons was no fool, and she knew when she was being sand-bagged. Hays and Plunkett had obviously discussed this, and had come to an agreement.

"I tell you what. If we can get enough on McCutcheon to close down this business with the bogus gold sales in Ireland, and the burglaries that go with it, and he is hung out to dry, then I'll go for it. I know just where to send Essig as well, where he'll be well taken care of for the next hundred years or so!" Lyons said.

"Good, Maureen. I knew we could rely on you for a pragmatic solution. Oh, and pass my congratulations on to the team for me. They have all done well, as you have yourself," Plunkett said.

"On that point, sir, Superintendent Hays and myself both believe that Sergeant Sally Fahy acted well above and beyond the call of duty, putting her own life at risk, in order to prevent further loss of life and bring Essig to justice," Lyons said. She was determined to milk the situation for all it was worth, given the concessions she had appeared to make.

"I hear you," Plunkett said. "I've been looking for a good candidate for a commendation from Mill Street in any case, just to show the boys up in Dublin we're not all bog men down here. Leave that one with me, and I'll look after it. God, detective, you strike a hard bargain!" he said, smiling.

"Thank you, sir, that will be very motivating for the whole team, and she really does deserve it," Lyons said.

"Away with you now, before I change my mind," Plunkett said. He took Lyons' empty coffee cup and put it on the tray, signalling that their meeting was over.

* * *

Lyons went back downstairs and was quickly followed by Mick Hays, who indicated that he needed to speak to her. They went into her office.

"That was brilliant, Maureen. You're some operator!" Hays said.

"Thanks. I think it might all work out, but I want to roast McCutcheon's balls. That poor wife of his is in bits. I don't blame the little Dutch tart. I doubt he pays them much, and she saw an opportunity and went for it," Lyons said.

"Crikey, remind me never to stray — not that I would ever, you understand."

"You have no idea, Mick. You think hell hath no fury – just see what happens when some eejit who thinks with his prick gets on the wrong side of me." And then, checking that there was no one observing, she went across the room to him and kissed him.

"Right, Sally and I are off to Westport to see the infamous Mr McCutcheon. Us girls are going to take him down!"

"God help the man, philanderer and all as he is. Don't let him buy you off with some gold bars."

"As if!"

* * *

Lyons collected Sally Fahy from the office and they drove out to Westport. On the way out, Lyons told Fahy a little of what had been discussed in Plunkett's office.

"The boys on mahogany row were well impressed with your actions in the jewellers, Sally," Lyons said.

"Ah, well, you know. I'm not in love with Eamon or anything, but I wouldn't like to see him with a big hole in the middle of his chest. He's not that bad! Have you handed in your gun yet? The guys in the basement were asking about it."

"No, not yet. In fact, I was thinking of keeping it. I'll have to get the permits sorted out and all that palaver, but things are getting rougher around here these days, and it might just come in handy to have it with me."

"Good idea. I'm sure Plunkett would sign it off. He thinks the world of you, you know."

"Go away out of that. He might if I was a man. Maybe I should change over – it's all the rage these days," she said, and the two girls burst out laughing.

"I really must protest, officer. You have my client here on the flimsiest of evidence, and he has spent quite an unpleasant night in the cells. I demand that you either charge him immediately, or release him. Do you understand?" O'Donnell said.

"Why don't you sit down and keep quiet until you have something sensible to say, Mr O'Donnell," Lyons said, and she took her seat alongside Fahy, facing McCutcheon.

"Now, Mr McCutcheon. We'll leave the adultery thing for the moment. Just now I'm more interested in how we found several hundred thousand euros worth of contraband gold in your storeroom. Would you care to tell us about it?" Lyons said.

"My client knows nothing about any gold, Inspector. He's never seen anything like that before. It's not his," O'Donnell said.

"I see. Well, not many people leave that kind of fortune just lying around for anyone to find. Would you care to speculate what it was doing in a consignment of tea towels addressed to your shop?"

"It must be something to do with the Lithuanian girls. They're all crooked – I don't know why I employ them," McCutcheon replied.

"You employ them because they are cheap and compliant, Mr McCutcheon, and occasionally you can get one or more of them into bed," Lyons said.

"Really, I must protest, Inspector. You can't speak to my client like that! Withdraw that remark."

Lyons ignored the man, and Sally Fahy asked the next question.

"Can you tell us, Mr McCutcheon, why those particular boxes were separated out from the rest of your stock and taken to your secret premises down by the harbour?"

"It's not a secret. There was no room in the main store. I use that place as an overflow facility."

"And a love nest, it seems. But when we checked your main store behind the shop, there was plenty of room for more stuff. So I'm afraid that doesn't make any sense," Fahy said.

"The stock moves very quickly. That's the whole idea behind Eurosaver. Fast turnover and small margins."

"My client has answered your question, Sergeant, now can we move on, please?" O'Donnell said.

Just then, Lyons' phone went off. She suspended the interview to take the call, seeing it was from Sinéad Loughran.

"Hi, Sinéad, what's up?"

Loughran told Lyons what they had discovered about the gold that had been found in McCutcheon's store.

When she had noted it all down, she went back in to the interview room.

"Mr McCutcheon, the gold bars that we discovered in your secret hiding place, camouflaged amongst a consignment of tea towels, have a smelter's mark on them," Lyons said.

"So?" McCutcheon said.

"The markings on the gold that we found on your premises are identical to the markings we found on a similar bar of gold that a woman by the name of Maria Geller was clutching in her dead hand after she was brutally murdered in one of your properties. Would you care to explain that to us?"

McCutcheon went bright red, and looked to O'Donnell for help, but O'Donnell just stared back po-faced and said nothing.

"Eh... eh, no c-comment," McCutcheon said. "But could I have a drink of water?"

"Certainly," Lyons said, and Fahy got up and left the room to fetch them all a drink.

"Mr McCutcheon, I would advise you to think very carefully about what you tell us next. It's clear that you are now implicated in the vicious killing of a foreign citizen, and that this gold that you pretend to know nothing about is somehow connected to that crime. If you don't have a very credible explanation, I'll be inclined to charge you with this woman's murder, along with all the other charges we have lined up for you. Do you understand?" Lyons said.

"Perhaps I could have a few minutes to confer with my client, Inspector?" O'Donnell interrupted.

"I'll give you ten minutes, and if he hasn't decided to tell us the truth when I come back in, I'll be charging him with at least one count of murder. Is that clear?" Lyons said. No one replied.

When Lyons left the room, she called John O'Connor.

"Anything, John?"

"Yes, loads. The stupid thing was barely secure at all. There are lots of emails from someone in Lithuania giving addresses and quantities of gold. And I've found some from China as well that appear to be advising details of shipments," O'Connor said.

"And these are definitely addressed to McCutcheon?"

"Yes, they are, and he's replied to some of them too, and signed the reply. There's banking details on here as well; I haven't had time to investigate that yet, but it looks like there's a lot of money sloshing around."

"Good work, John. Keep at it. I think we've nearly cracked him," she said.

Chapter Twenty-one

When Lyons returned to the interview room with Sally Fahy, McCutcheon's demeanour had changed completely. His wiry little solicitor was the first to speak.

"My client is prepared to co-operate with you fully with regard to the gold, but he wishes to make it clear that he had nothing whatever to do with any murder, or any other violent crime. We trust due consideration will be given to the fulness of his co-operation in the event that you bring lesser charges."

"Let's see what he has to say first, shall we?" Lyons said.

"It all started two years ago when I was in China on a buying trip. I go every year to see the latest products they have that are suitable for Eurosaver, and to meet my suppliers. I was at a dinner with some of them one night in a swanky hotel, and one of the men broached the subject of gold with me. He told me that they were selling quite a bit of the stuff by mail order over the internet in Ireland, and asked if I would be prepared to become a local distributor. He said it made things easier and quicker if the gold could be posted to the customers locally. I said I might be, and he went on to tell me how it worked. They would ship the gold over in with some of the other stuff I was buying, and mark the cartons that had gold in them with a specific Chinese symbol. Then, they would email me the names and addresses of their customers, and all I had to do was to post the correct quantity of gold to the customer from Westport, and I would receive a handsome commission. Money for nothing, as they say," McCutcheon said.

"But you must have realised that it was dodgy, I mean, was the gold declared to customs?" Fahy said.

"No, of course not. The goods were described as household linens."

"So, you admit to defrauding the State of import duties and VAT as far as these illicit imports are concerned?" Fahy said.

"Yes, yes, I suppose so."

"And were you aware that the gangs that were providing you with the names and addresses of their customers were also arranging to have the gold stolen back from the same customers and sent back to the source?" Fahy said.

"No, of course not. I knew nothing about that," McCutcheon said.

"What did you know of Maria Geller?" Lyons took over the questioning.

"Very little. She booked 22 Owen Glen from me on Airbnb once, or maybe twice, that's all."

"Have you ever heard the names Matis Vitkus or Dieter Essig?"

"No, never. Who are they?"

"Never mind. Tell me, Mr McCutcheon, how much did you make from this little enterprise of yours?" Lyons said.

"Just a few grand. Pocket money really."

"We'll see about that. We're going through your various bank accounts right now, so we'll have a good idea how much pocket money you have collected very shortly. Right, I'm suspending this interview for now. We'll reconvene at five o'clock, and we will be charging you Mr McCutcheon, you can be sure of that."

* * *

While Fahy and Lyons had been interviewing McCutcheon in Westport, Flynn had been busy with Essig, accompanied by Janssen. They informed Essig that as there were a number of Europol warrants out for him, there was a possibility that he could be deported, but that in order for this to happen, he would have to fully co-operate with the Gardaí so that they could clear up the local events.

Essig consulted his solicitor, and agreed that this was probably the best course of action for him, especially if he could convince Janssen to reduce the current charges to manslaughter which carried a maximum sentence of fifteen years.

Janssen said that he could possibly agree to that, if Essig was co-operative, and could show that he did not set out to kill the woman.

"Maria Geller was a courier for an organisation that recycles gold, stealing it back from the customers who they sold it to. Geller travels around Europe collecting the gold, and brings it back to Eastern Europe where it is melted down and re-sold. But we had information that she was

187

skimming off some for her own benefit. The organisation can't allow that for obvious reasons, so they sent me to see her. At first, we got on well. Very well. But then when I talked about her habit, she became very angry and threatened me with the knife. I managed to get it from her, and in the struggle she got stabbed. So I took her gold, and fled, and took her phone, her keys and computer too. Later, I came back to see if I could find the gold she had in the house, but I had no luck," Essig said.

"There's one thing that's been bothering me from the start. Why did you throw Geller's keys out at the side of the road?" Flynn said.

"I realised that I had probably left my fingerprints on the key thing, and maybe small traces of Geller's blood too, so I got rid of them. I didn't think they would be found."

"And what about the cord around her neck?" Flynn said.

"Once I realised that she was dead, I did that. It is a sign to others in the organisation not to get greedy. They know it."

"OK. So what about Matis Vitkus – was his death an accident too?" Flynn said.

"It was also self-defence. We got into a fight about how he had come to sell the phone and computer with advertisements. It was crazy. Of course the police would be watching. He has a bad temper. He had a knife under his pillow, and he brought it out. I thought he was going to stab me, so I had to shoot. I'm really sorry – he did not need to die like that. He had been a good friend up till then."

* * *

By late in the afternoon, John O'Connor had harvested a mass of information from McCutcheon's computer. His efforts revealed that McCutcheon had almost half a million euro stashed in various accounts, most of them overseas. It was clear that the scam had been going on for some time, and that quite a large amount of gold had passed through McCutcheon's hands.

Lyons called Hays to discuss with him how they should proceed.

"Does any of this link McCutcheon to the murders?" Hays said.

"No. All we can prove with all this stuff is that he was in receipt of gold from China without going through Customs and without paying import taxes and VAT. Of course he also received orders for the product that were relayed from the website, packaged it up and posted it out, which may involve him in further VAT fraud, but that's it," Lyons said.

"Do you not think it's a bit of a coincidence that Maria Geller was staying in one of his units, and she just happened to be heavily involved herself?" Hays said.

"I guess. But from an evidence point of view, that's all it is – just a coincidence. There's nothing that ties the two of them together apart from the holiday bookings."

"OK, but you know what we both think about coincidences."

"Yes, I agree, but without something more concrete that's all we've got on him. Anyway, he's going to get sufficient punishment one way or the other," Lyons said.

"How do you figure that out?"

"We told his wife that he was found in bed with the Dutch girl. She had no idea. I got the impression she wouldn't be hanging around. And their house isn't even in his name – presumably another tax dodge. So he could be sleeping on the streets in a few weeks."

"Right, well, you better charge him with the fraud stuff and bail him. And keep your head down for a while then – as I said, he reckons he's connected. Are you sure there's nothing else we can get him on?" Hays said.

"I really don't think so. I don't want him to walk either, but without hard evidence…"

"OK. Well, at least we have Essig. I need to speak to Plunkett about him. I'm not sure what he wants done with him."

"OK. Let me know. Janssen wants to take him back to Utrecht."

"Right, thanks. Chat later," Hays said.

* * *

Hays went to see Plunkett, and they agreed that the best outcome would be for Janssen to take Essig back to the Netherlands.

"Have we managed to close down the whole operation, do you think, Mick?" Plunkett said.

"We will do. There's enough information on McCutcheon's computer to get right inside the entire thing. But I'm inclined to hand that over to the Fraud Squad. It would take too much of our time and resources to try and unravel it all," Hays said.

"Sounds about right."

"Do you think McCutcheon will cause trouble for us?" Hays said.

"I doubt it. Even our politicians won't want to be anywhere near something as tricky as this. They'll dump him once they hear what he's been up to."

"Will you be able to plant the word in the right ears, sir?" Hays said.

"Now you know better than to ask me that, Mick. But, yes, of course I will."

* * *

McCutcheon was charged with several crimes related to VAT; excise duties and income tax. He was then given bail, and told to report to Westport Garda station twice weekly, and to surrender his passport. He left the station in the company of his solicitor feeling very sorry for himself.

Flynn had made arrangements with the Customs and Excise people and the Revenue Commissioners to move in on Eurosaver and seize all the stock. The shop would be closed down: it looked as if McCutcheon had been undervaluing the cost of the merchandise he was importing from China for the purpose of reducing his tax liability. He could owe literally millions in taxes; duties and penalties, and the authorities were not going to risk the assets being removed.

Chapter Twenty-two

Janssen and Flynn had some further interviews with Dieter Essig. He gave up some of the information relating to the operation he was involved in to Janssen, and he in turn passed this on to his colleagues in Utrecht. The Dutch police reckoned they had enough information to round up at least some of the gang, and disrupt their operations considerably.

Lyons met Janssen in the open plan where he was busy emailing details to the Netherlands.

"Hi. Have you got enough information from your man, do you think?" she said.

"I think he has given as much as he is prepared to tell us for now. It has been most useful. My colleagues in Utrecht have arrested ten people already and seized several computers and files."

"Great. Any news on the Chinese connection?" Lyons said.

"That is much more difficult. The best we can hope is that we intercept some shipments before they change their methods, and the gang get fed up losing such a lot of money and turn their hand to some other business."

"Can you not get co-operation from the Chinese authorities?" Lyons asked.

"It's very difficult. It's not that they don't want to help, but the language is a challenge, the place is so huge, and much of the industry is carried out in tiny workshops in the back streets. And of course, no one wants to disrupt the legitimate business of China's gold production. That would be very serious. Did you know they are becoming the biggest exporters of gold in the world?" Janssen said.

"No, I didn't know that. Anyway, when do you want to take Essig back?"

"I have been speaking to my boss. He wants me back tomorrow if we can arrange it."

"Yes, of course. I'll get someone to set it up. We might be able to provide a plain clothes detective from Dublin to accompany you to Amsterdam. Would that be helpful?" Lyons said.

"Oh, yes, that would be very helpful, thank you Maureen. Will you come to the airport?"

"No, I'm afraid not. I'm very busy here. But we will arrange a secure van for Essig and an armed escort right to the steps of the plane. Oh, and you may have to travel first class to stay away from the other passengers. It will be a scheduled flight."

"I think I can handle that. Before I forget, my boss wants to send his thanks to you personally for all you have done, and I would like to thank you too for your hospitality. You have been very kind. If ever you are in Utrecht, I hope I can repay you," Janssen said.

"Now, I might just take you up on that someday, Luuk."

Epilogue

Dieter Essig and Luuk Janssen, accompanied by two detectives from Dublin, flew to Amsterdam in the first class section of the Aer Lingus scheduled flight. They were met by the Dutch Police at the Schiphol, who drove Essig back to Utrecht. He was charged with two counts of murder to go along with the several other charges that he had accumulated whilst he had been on the run. In preparation for his trial, a considerable amount of evidence was supplied by the Galway Gardaí, and Eamon Flynn and Sally Fahy travelled to the Netherlands to give evidence of his arrest at the trial. The jury found him guilty, and the judge, unusually for the Netherlands, sentenced him to a whole of life term in prison.

Batty McCutcheon was successfully pursued by the tax authorities. All of his assets were seized, and his business was closed down. The Eurosaver shop in Westport was boarded up, and remains so. It took the investigators over a year to disentangle McCutcheon's affairs and take possession of the cash that he had hidden away in various overseas banks. His house and the property in Owen Glen were part of the seizure, so by the time he came to court he was surviving on benefits and living in a hostel for the homeless – a converted hotel near Sligo. Eleanor McCutcheon never returned to Westport. She purchased a house in the suburbs of Dublin for cash, where she is still living today.

Agnes Greely found other holiday cottages to clean in Owen Glen, but she didn't venture into the private lettings business anymore.

Matis Vitkus was buried by the local council in Galway following a sombre funeral service. There were no mourners present to hear the priest say mass for the man, and he ended up in an unmarked grave in the local cemetery.

Birchall's jewellers featured extensively in the news coverage of the events that had taken place there, and turnover increased by nearly thirty percent, much to the delight of the owner.

Chief Superintendent Plunkett followed through on the issue of an award for Sally Fahy, and along with a handful of other brave members of the force, she was presented with a commendation by the Commissioner at a ceremony at Garda Headquarters in the Phoenix Park in Dublin. The rest of the team were in attendance, and helped Fahy to celebrate in fine style long into the small hours.

The efforts of the Gardaí, the Dutch Police and the tax authorities put an end to the gold scam that had been going on in Ireland for some time. Irish people continue to buy gold in quite substantial quantities from legitimate dealers – it always has been a safe haven, and helps greatly in avoiding death duties when people pass on – but it is no longer stolen back by the very people who sell it.

Character List

Chief Superintendent Finbarr Plunkett – the politically motivated ultimate head of the Galway detectives.

Superintendent Mick Hays – finally settling into his new role, and leaving most of the operational duties to the team led by his partner.

Senior Inspector Maureen Lyons – the feisty Garda who is also Hays' partner and is known for her somewhat unconventional methods.

Detective Sergeant Eamon Flynn – an observant and tenacious Garda who never lets go.

Detective Sergeant Sally Fahy – an ex-civilian worker who loves police work.

Detective Garda Mary Costelloe – a new member of the team who shows great promise.

Detective Garda Liam Walsh – recently promoted from the uniformed ranks. Will he make the grade?

Garda John O'Connor – the unit's tech savvy assistant who loves to explore computers and mobile phones to reveal evidence.

Sinéad Loughran – the forensic team leader with a good nose for wrongdoing.

Garda Peadar Tobin – a good-looking young Garda with chivalrous tendencies who needs to earn some extra money.

Sergeant Séan Mulholland – a wily old Garda who runs the station in Clifden in his own unique way.

Dr Julian Dodd – an excellent pathologist with a rather superior attitude.

Inspector Luuk Janssen – a Dutch police officer who wants to do more than observe the goings-on in Ireland.

Matis Vitkus – a low level criminal from Eastern Europe.

Maria Geller – a frequent visitor to Ireland who takes in more that the scenery.

Agnes Greely – a cleaner with a lucrative side-line.

Dieter Essig – part of an organised crime gang from Lithuania and The Netherlands.

Batty McCutcheon – a businessman from Westport who has some unusual business interests.

Eleanor McCutcheon – Batty McCutcheon's long-suffering wife.

Ineke – an attractive Dutch girl and shop worker.

Rami – a Lithuanian shop girl.

Teresa Birchall – the owner of a jeweller's shop in Galway.

Cecil O'Donnell – a solicitor.

Mr Mulvaney – another solicitor.

Deirdre MacAllister – a member of the forensic team.

If you enjoyed this book, please let others know by leaving a quick review on Amazon. Also, if you spot anything untoward in the paperback, get in touch. We strive for the best quality and appreciate reader feedback.

editor@thebookfolks.com

www.thebookfolks.com

BOOKS BY DAVID PEARSON

All available free with Kindle Unlimited, in paperback and many as audiobooks.

For Detective Inspector Aidan Burke, policing
Dublin's streets is a duty, but protecting his officers
comes first. That provides a good environment for
promising detectives like DS Fiona Moore to grow.
As this series of murder mysteries set in the
metropolitan but at times parochial city and its
surroundings progresses, we see Moore tackle difficult
and dangerous cases with a good success rate. As
Burke himself rises in rank, they become a formidable
crime fighting duo.

35836563R00125